Windy John's Me 'n Tut

I Promise, Daddy, I Promise

Joyce Rapier

AmErica House
Baltimore

© 2002 by Joyce Rapier.

All rights reserved. No part of this book may be reproduced in any form without written permission from the publishers, except by a reviewer who may quote brief passages in a review to be printed in a newspaper or magazine.

First printing

ISBN: 1-59129-153-4
PUBLISHED BY AMERICA HOUSE
BOOK PUBLISHERS
www.publishamerica.com
Baltimore
Printed in the United States of America

Dedication

In loving memory to my Daddy,
better known as "Windy John"

and in honor of my husband, Dan,
who encouraged me to write these stories.

Acknowledgment to my Daddy, "Windy John"

To you, Daddy:

I salute your ability to create joy and happiness with stories from your childhood. Daddy was a natural born "Story Teller" and could concoct the most outlandish, wild-eyed tales ever told. He left the listener wondering if the stories were fact or fiction.

Daddy told of how he and his best friend, Tut, met. They grew up together, practically lived together and were almost glued at the hips. You couldn't find one of them without the other one being in a close proximity.

Daddy enjoyed life, learning new things and telling people about it. In fact, his nickname was "Windy John." He worked at the smelter, had a license to deal firearms, was a part-time sheriff when needed, was a constable, and finally, after many years of hard work, retired from the Missouri Pacific Railroad.

Aged and unable to care for himself, he decided to live in a nursing home. Each day I would visit him and request stories from his youth to help keep his mind active. Since Daddy wasn't in the best of health and sometimes not in a frame of mind to recall times, places, or ages of those he was telling about, his eyes would light up. On occasion he would drift asleep while trying to tell the stories and be unable to continue the tales he loved so much to tell, or get confused while in mid-sentence and end the story before it began. Sometimes he would roll with laughter before he began a story. Although the stories won't be in chronological order, I told Daddy to begin his stories as though he was sitting among all of his old cronies, spinning yarns from his impressive years. "After all, Daddy," I said, "they don't call you 'Windy John' for nothing!" He smiled, laughed real hard and the stories began….

Let's Sit and Jaw Fer A Spell

Howdee! Y'all best pull up a soft spot, lean back and pretend you're caught up in a time warp, 'cause I'm going to conjure up in your mind beautiful pictures of long ago and some of the most wonderful tales ever told. Some of the one-line quips I mention were often spoken by Pa and Ma. The stories, though, are from mere observations and stupid foolhardy experiences.

A few of these stories might be a mere figment of my imagination. It will be up to y'all to figure out which tales are the truth and ponder if the remainder are fiction, border on complete stupidity or just maybe skirt with the ridiculous. Picture the early 1900's, hilly northwestern section of Northern Crawford County in Arkansas.

By the way, I do have an education. There's no Ph.D. written beside my name, and no extraordinary schooling did I complete. You might say I have the M.H.K. (Master of Hard Knocks) written on my forehead. If I began to speak with a few foreign words, such as iffen, nary, bodacious, airy, you'enses, jawin', or any such words that run together, think nothing of it. None of these words are from another country. They're simply hill talk or pure hillbilly jargon from my past. For me, well, it seems so naturally unpretentious; I simply can't erase the speech from my mind or from my tongue.

I am about to bend your ears with tales of yesterday, and since we haven't been introduced, I am reminded and think often of my Pa and Ma's profound words:

"J D., this is sich a small ol' werld. Why, I reckon iffen Adam un Eve started all this here heap'o people, some whar down th' line we'uns er kin ta jist about everyone what draws air 'er spits chawin' terbakkie."

Ma would chime in, "It's a fact, son, ye jist cain't git away frum th' beginnin'. Thar will always be a beginnin, even iffen we pass ta our rewards ta find th' golden shore, thar'll be new life, new seasins, un a reasin fer livin'."

Pa and Ma were God-fearing people and loved the very essence of living. Every morning was a new experience for them. Very few times have I encountered my Pa or Ma with a frown on their face or a bad word to say about any living creature, human or otherwise.

Just talking about my Pa and Ma gives me immeasurable warmth and tenderness. They taught me purity of love, creation at its best, unselfishness, and the quality of life which God held for each of us in the palm of His hand. All we had to do was reach out, trust and believe in our choices, hold our heads up high and be proud of who we are.

Ready? Pay attention! It's ear burnin' time.

The Beginning

When Pa and Ma came to the holler, they had nothing but the wagon, team of horses and all the stuff necessary to set up the beginnings of a homestead. There wasn't much level land to speak of, except for a part of forty acres. These forty acres seemed to be God sent. Pa and Ma had traveled for many weeks in search of a place to lay their roots. It seemed as though they would never find the right spot. Quite frankly, if they hadn't settled in the holler, I wouldn't be telling you these stories.

Pa decided to set down their roots, right here and now! No more traveling, no more wondering if they had been right in leaving all their siblings and parents in another part of the country or thinking of "what if's" or "what might have beens." These forty acres would be the perfect spot.

As Ma and Pa walked over the land, feeling the soil beneath their feet, smelling the sweet perfume of pine and cedar, they knew, with God's help and a lot of hard work, it was the right place. They selected a perfect section of the land for the house. The house would be log. Plenty of hardwood trees were waiting just for that purpose.

Before they began to fell the trees, Ma drew a plan for the house. The front of the house would face south to catch the winter sun. The entire house would be like a "shotgun" house: if a body had a mind to, he could stand at the front door, shoot a gun straight down the middle of the house and watch as the bullets exited through the opened back door. Living and eating quarters on one side, a bedroom on the other.

The front porch would be large, with high log beams for support. When you walked through the front door, it opened to a very wide living area. It would be a gathering place for family and friends to sit around, play music and enjoy the warmth of the hearth.

At the opposite end would be the kitchen. The kitchen would have a big wood stove for cooking and tables. Plenty of tables to prepare fresh apple pies, breads and goodies. Maybe even a pantry!

Ma wanted two bedrooms but settled for one. A bedroom didn't need to be very large—just large enough to have an old iron bed and maybe a chiffonier. A chifferobe, as they pronounced it, was usually made of cedar and used as a clothes closet or a place for quilts. Mostly though, since we didn't have a lot of clothes, we just hung 'em on wood pegs. By the way, the door for the bedroom was just a curtain. Above the bedroom was a loft, big enough for us kids to sleep. In the hot summer, Ma would use the loft to store stuff and we would get to sleep in the big room on pallets. But in the wintertime, she'd let us kids shinny up a straight ladder that had been nailed in place, and we would cozy down for the night. We'd all turn over at the same time to keep warm. Since there was no insulation in the house, the wintertime got mighty cold.

Pa told how he and Ma would fell the trees one by one and hone out the planks for the house. It took a long while because building a log house was very hard on the body and very time consuming. Each log had to be placed just right with notches wherever a supporting beam connected. That was for settling of the old logs because over time the house would shift and soon be in a heap of rubble. Then came the mud chinking in all the spaces between the logs. Finding the right kind of dirt, which needed to be clay, and mixing it to the right consistency was rough on the hands and took its toll on the body.

One evening while Ma and Pa were resting from their hard day's work, a man named Elias Ellison came riding onto the premises. Mr. Ellison was a big, stout man, nearly seven feet tall and clearly pushing old age, or so they thought. Proper manners didn't allow for asking a person's age or being disrespectful. His eyes were steel gray and his hair was long. His beard was rather white and bushy with the faint glow of tobacco stains around the creases of his mouth. Inside his hair, resting atop his ear, was a corncob pipe still whispering faint streams of smoke. This gentleman was a formidable sight. Pa and Ma weren't quite sure if they were in imminent danger, having just met a real live Goliath.

When Mr. Ellison dismounted his horse and came toward Ma and Pa, he stuck out his hand and said, "I am Elias Ellison. I hold deed ta this here propity and what'cha think yore doin'? Don'cha know better'n to let this woman heft all them logs? Iffen you needed help, why, all ye had ta do was yell. Th' hills'er jist full'o men what can heave logs through th' air. Iffen you'ens woud'da tolled th' bell down at the general store, why, ye woud'da been a swarm with hard werkin' bodies."

Ma and Pa just stood there with their mouths gaped wide open, at a total loss for words. They weren't aware of a living soul in these parts, let alone a bell at a general store.

Mr. Ellison said, "Whut'sa matter you folks? Ain't airy one of ye able ta tok?"

Ma and Pa began to laugh and cry at the same time. Pa said, "Well, Mr. Ellison, we shore didn't figger this land beholded ta somebody else. Iffen we'd knowed this here land was'a dun solt, we'uns never would'a laid down'er bed roll."

Ma began to cry 'cause she knew they would have to pack everything and leave for new beginnings. Mr. Ellison patted her on the back and wiped her tears with a slightly soiled old kerchief and said, "Not to worrie, Missie, I figger nary no harm's dun. Why, I reckon you'ins jist done me un my missus a big faver. Ya see, we'us gittin on up in yars un cain't do th' werk we use'ta do. Er' daughter is miles away frum here, un we reckon iffen she ever gits back to th' holler, she won't have any need fer th' likes of th' land. When Jennie growed fully, she left th' holler ta make her way in th' world. We'uns git a letter ever now'en then sayin' she done met a man ta marrie un how they'us doin. I reckon she knows we love'er but I figger in my heart we shore nuff won't ever git ta see her or her offspring. I will give this here land to you'ens, help with th' raisin of th' house and help git ye settled. All I ask of ye in return is ta take care of my missus, iffen th' good Lord takes me to my reward un leaves her without any help."

Ma and Pa were flabbergasted! The first body they meet scares them to death, is a nonstop talker, and gives them land? Their guardian angel was surely working overtime.

They swore to Mr. Ellison that his missus would never be left alone or without the help she needed. From that moment on, the four of them were an "adopted" family.

Pa listened and learned from Mr. Ellison. Although Pa could do just about anything, Mr. Ellison's words and deeds were profound and meaningful, and Ma learned how to can goods, spin yarn and search for the berries and roots to dye homespun cloth. Ma made soap out of hog lard and lye and scrubbed clothes on an old wooden scrub board. Pa and Ma learned everything about living from the goodness of the Ellisons' hearts and generous gift of the land.

Within a year, with the help of Mr. Ellison and some of the hill folk, the log house was complete. Since Ma and Pa didn't have too much time to themselves after they settled in the hollers, all the local hill folk did a charivari, with pots and pans and anything that made noise. All night long the people rejoiced and when sun came up, they disappeared into the hills. That night Ma and Pa were alone for the first time in a year. The house had been completed, the deed was given to Pa for the land, and all the house needed was a family to make it a home.

Nine months later, Effie Mae entered this world. Effie was

short for Evaline and Mae was the given name of Grammaw Ellison. Effie Mae was the prettiest little baby. Her hair was black like Ma's and her eyes were cool blue. Grandma Ellison said she had the longest legs and could kick the brains outta arie soul who dared to mess with her. Effie Mae was a feisty little thing and stayed the baby until Aunt Sukie came along twelve months later.

Aunt Sukie is a name I gave her cause I couldn't pronounce Anna Sulee. Aunt Sukie looked more like Pa than Ma. Her hair was golden blonde and looked like spun silk. Her complexion was that of Pa. Olive-skinned, square-cut chin, dimples, and dark blue eyes: She was a real natural beauty.

Then, lo and behold, I was born. I was named John Dean, "J.D." for short. Grammaw Ellison said the J. D. stood for "jist devilish." I looked somewhat like Ma and a whole lot like Pa. Trouble is, nobody could ever figure out who I favored. One minute I looked exactly like Pa and the next minute someone would say, "Ye look jist like yore Ma." As far as I was concerned, I looked like me. Anyway, within three years, Ma and Pa had a family to make their house a home.

Grammaw and Grampaw

Grammaw and Grampaw Ellison, as we all called them, were the pure salt of the earth. They weren't my blood kin relatives but adopted grandparents. I loved them dearly.

I remember sitting on Grampaw's lap, falling asleep with my head resting on his long white whiskers. He smelled of fresh new air and lye soap. His clean clothes smelled like sunshine pouring over rain-soaked land.

Two of his bad habits? The fondness for "chawin' terbakkie" and pipe "terbakkie." His hobby: carving!

Grampaw would sit on the front porch, whistle a funny little tune, then spit. His jaw was pooched out with a plug of the nastiest, black old leaves I ever did see. One jaw would get tired from holding the plug and he'd switch it to the other side. Pretty soon he'd pucker up his lips, purse them real tight and spit the juice. The place where all the spit landed was stained with years of terbakkie juice. Nothing grew there, either! Didn't have a chance! You could always find Grampaw—just follow the fresh spit.

When Grampaw got tired of the "plug," out came the corncob pipe. Grampaw would whittle down a corncob to "jist th' right size," hollow out the center and poke a hole in the side for the pipe stem. Before he'd smoke it, he'd soak it in water for a few days. "Thet's jist so's I don't burn my whiskers," he'd remind me. Then he'd shake out the water, cram terbakkie leaves down in the hollowed-out center, lift up a piece of burning kindling, put the hot burning end on the terbakkie leaves, and breathe real deep. Pretty soon, the tobacco would start smoldering. Grampaw wouldn't smoke it just then. He would set the pipe down and let the terbakkie leaves cure the hollowed-out corncob. How he kept from choking to death was beyond me! I could never master his conquest, but that's another story. I'll tell you about that later!

Little wooden creatures, figures of men, women and children, birdhouses, whirlygigs and thingamajiggs were Grampaw's favorite pastime. He would find the gnarliest piece of wood and whittle away. Fine-tuning every feature of the face with masterful precision or making a wild animal carving come to life was fascinating. "Been werkin' all my life, sun up ta sun down. I aim ta n'joy my chaw un whittlin."

Oh, how I loved my Grampaw. He was one of a kind.

Grammaw was just the opposite of Grampaw. That is, in temperament! Grampaw was mild-mannered and laid back. Grammaw? Well now, if she had a mind to, she could strip the bark off a tree with her tongue, spit it in a pile and have fire shooting from it in a matter of seconds. She scared the dickens out of me! I knew not to cross Grammaw and to give her a wide berth when she was on the warpath. "Hell hath no fury like a woman scorned" should have been her middle name!

On the other side, Grammaw was a hard worker, smart, and dipped snuff! She knew every kind of poisonous and nonpoisonous berry, tree, snake, and critter that lurked in the holler. She'd say, "Git thet stuff outta yer mouff. Thet stuff'll draw yore toenails up in yer liver" or "git away frum thet, it'll lay'a bite on ye un rotten up yer blud. Ye'll stink afore we'cun git ye berried!"

Grammaw always spoke her mind. Speaking her mind is why she and Grampaw didn't build on the lower forty. "Nope. Ye ain't gittin' me in thet hole. Ye ain't a pokin' me whar th' crek's a'gonna rise'tup. We's plantin' er feet ta th' high ground. Iffen I have a mind ta, I be a wantin' ta see whut's croachin' fer miles." Sure enough, Grampaw gave in and settled on the hilliest part of the holler.

Grammaw loved the outdoors. She loved to cook beans in a big crusted pot on an open fire outside the front stoop. She had a cook stove in the house but "liked the smell" of the beans cooking outside. She'd throw a chunk of salt pork in the beans and let them simmer till the bean juice was almost thick as gravy. Anyone within smelling distance would know where they could get a good meal. Grammaw would bring out the pewter plates, eating utensils, a plate of the biggest sourdough biscuits, freshly picked wild onions, strips of fried jowl and fresh churned butter. We'd slather those sourdoughs with golden butter, sop the biscuits in the beans, mix in wild onions and jowl and chow down. "Um, um, um, yore a good cooker Grammaw," we'd hum in unison. Oh, how I'd love to sit on Grammaw's porch right now and have a big plate of her fixins.

Every Monday morning, the old black iron kettle would be surrendering the aroma of lye soap and lavender. Grammaw would stoke the fire beneath the pot until the embers were so hot you could feel the heat ten feet away. Smoke would billow in the air, then float gently down the holler.

Grammaw would take the lye soap, rub it hard down the ripples of a scrub board, and make lots of bubbles, submerge the clothes, pound them with a heavy stick and then, one by one, scrub until the clothes were clean. Grammaw Ellison would pour some bluing in the rinse water in hopes of getting her fresh new wash the color of white puffy clouds. I guess that was because the old well water was full of iron and had a tendency to make the clothes a tinge of yellow ocher.

In my mind, I can picture the metal clothesline wire strung through two trees and propped up by a long skinny pole with notches in the end to support the wire. Clothes swaying in the gentle breeze while songbirds perched precariously on the wooden clothespins made Grammaw smile with pride.

Have you ever had thoughts of the past, captured everlasting pictures in your mind, remembered scents, sweet aromas and have the feeling of being surrounded by "something special"?

Grampaw's gentle touch while I was sleeping on his long white whiskers, the smell of his chaw terbakkie, his corncob pipe and watching his long fingers caress the wooden carvings, along with Grammaw's "smoked beans," smelling a new Monday wash and remembering her sayings…That's my "something special."

Jennie

I think I was just about five years old when Jennie, the daughter of Grammaw and Grampaw Ellison, came home. She was going to have another baby and needed help with the birthing.

A man dropped her and her little boy, named Tut, off at Mr. Matlock's general store and took off in the opposite direction. Poor old Jennie and Tut had to walk four miles to get to Grammaw's house and barely got there before she went into labor.

Grampaw saw Jennie and Tut coming up the path. He hollered for Grammaw and they ran down the path to meet 'em. Jennie collapsed into Grampaw's arms and he carried her on up to the house.

Grammaw took Tut by the hand and said, "Why, youngin' ye must be at least nigh on ta four yar old. Ya must be my lil' Tut. Yore Ma telled us about ya in one'a her letters."

Tut looked at Grammaw and said, "Thar's sumthin' wrong wiff my Ma. Do ya think ya can fix'er?"

"I'll shore nuff do my best, God help me, I'll do my best."

Jennie was in labor for one whole day and night. Her screaming and hollering would echo down the hollers with a ghostly haunt. Jennie was becoming delirious with pain and would go in and out of consciousness. It was apparent to Ma that Jennie hadn't eaten in quite a while. Her arms and legs were thin and her face was drawn. The alluring luster had faded from her long auburn hair. Her once-vivid blue eyes were sunk deeply into shallow pockets, forcing her cheekbones to jut out in prominence. Ma had gone to help Grammaw Ellison for the duration of labor and would stay at Grammaw's for as long as need be.

While Ma and Grammaw were tending Jennie, Grampaw and Pa took care of all us kids. Tut and Grampaw went to our house since Ma needed to devote her time to Jennie and helping Grammaw. She didn't want any of us kids to be there during the labor, chasing around the house. Pa and Grampaw agreed. They would make sure we were fed properly and do the chores usually performed by Ma. Grampaw told Ma to take the "cow horn" off the mantle and blow it when the baby was born. He'd be there as soon as the signal was given.

Jennie had worn herself completely down from trying to give birth. At long last the baby came into this world. Her little body was all wrinkled and looked so pitiful. The hair on top of her head was the color of red ripe cherries. Ma said her skin was white as ewe's wool and her eyes were dark brown. She didn't weigh more than an armfull of apples but made up for it in length. It amazed Ma and Grammaw how this little baby girl was as healthy as she was, let alone curled up for so long in poor little emaciated Jennie.

Grammaw proudly raised the newborn baby in the air announced to God, "We's goin' ta name this here lil' baby Della Jo. Help us, Lord, ta be th' kinda people ta teach her th' way of your doins'."

While Ma cleaned up the bedroom and put fresh wearing clothes on Jennie, Grammaw cleaned baby Jo and wrapped her in one of the blankets belonging to Jennie when she was a baby. Grammaw prepared a bottle of warm cow's milk, and baby Jo began to suckle. Baby Jo would suckle a bottle like there was no tomorrow and couldn't seem to get enough milk in her system to last more than thirty minutes. Jennie couldn't nurse her because she was so weak and frail.

Grammaw always hoped for grandchildren and was beaming with pride as she laid baby Jo in Jennie's arms. Jennie could barely hold the baby but managed to bend down and kiss her tiny forehead. That made Grammaw cry. Jennie really loved her baby, but she knew in her heart she would never see her baby grow to a woman.

Ma went to the mantle, took down the "cow horn," walked to the front porch and blew it. The sound filtering from the wide open end of the horn sounded somewhat like a cow in distress. It was around six o'clock in the morning when Ma sounded the horn.

The only thing stirring in the holler at six o'clock in the morning is an occasional rooster waking his hens or crickets and frogs. Pa and Grampaw were already awake, sitting on the front porch drinking coffee when they heard the "cow horn." Pa went to the barn, saddled Old Joe, Grampaw's horse, and led him back to the house. Grampaw took off for the mile or so ride.

When Grampaw got home, Ma was waiting on the porch for him. She told him about the torture Jennie went through and that it "looked bad for Jennie." Ma said Grampaw sunk to the ground on his knees, held his face with his large hands and sobbed. After regaining his composure, he went to Jennie's bedside, knelt on his knees and prayed. Jennie took her frail little hand and patted Grampaw on the head. "It's gonna be okay, Pa. Th' good Lord's lookin' down rite now. I love you un Ma." With that, she mustered up what strength she had and kissed Pa. Pa was so overcome with grief that he needed to get some air. He walked outside so Jennie could rest. It was sad, but Grammaw, Ma and Grampaw knew the end was near for Jennie.

Before Jennie died, she asked Ma to come to her side. She swore Ma to secrecy! What she was about to tell Ma must never be told, but Jennie was unaware of Grampaw Ellison standing outside the bedroom window. Jennie grabbed Ma's hand and revealed the secret. The man who brought her to the hills wasn't her husband, but a kindly old man who found them walking on the old gravel road as she and Tut were returning home. The man she married just up and ran off. She had no idea where he was and if he would ever come back. Because times were hard, she knew she wouldn't be able to take care of Tut and a new baby. It was impossible to find decent work, take care of Tut and be a new mother without some kind of help. She pondered what to do, right up to the time she was ready to give birth. The only solution to her problem was to get back home to her Ma and Pa. "Jist tell everyone thet me'n Tut wus comin' home ta visit. Don't tell'em about my husband runnin' off."

She made Ma promise that when Tut and baby Jo were left alone in this world, they would be taken care of and given the love she wouldn't be able to give them. Ma promised Jennie that Tut and baby Jo would never be without a family, but sometime in the future, when they started asking questions, they would be told the truth. The truth was always better than a lie because the truth, although it may hurt for awhile, heals naturally, but lies, no matter how big or small, dig deep into the heart and create wounds that may never heal. Jennie understood what Ma was saying and knew without question that Ma was a good woman.

Grampaw heard everything and rushed in the room with tears streaming down his face. Grief was drawn upon his tanned skin as he held Jennie in his arms. Grammaw came into the room just before Jennie died. Grammaw and Grampaw told Jennie how much they loved her and would take care of Tut and baby Jo.

Grampaw never told Ma what he overheard, and Ma never told Grampaw. Each of them thought the secret would never be told.

Last Respects

Haunting memories of a dead person laying in rest in a living room gives me the willies! I think...(Daddy took a long pause)......I might have been only five years old, or maybe a little younger at the time. I can't really remember how old I was, but I can vividly recall the atmosphere of people and the smell of food that permeated every crevice within breathing distance.

When Jennie died, Ma prepared the "laying" room. At the time, I thought everyone would be having a big old sleepover on pallets thrown on the floor. Every now and then when there was lots of work to be done, some of the hill folk would bring food and drink and spend the night in the "laying" room. The following morning everyone would get up at the crack of dawn to help with the labor. Sometimes the labor would be harvesting crops, laying by the wood for winter, mending rock fences, quilting, canning or any other thing a mind could conjure.

No siree! Not this time! Jennie was stuck in the laying room all by herself. That was just fine by me. Up to this point in my life I had never seen a dead body and didn't want any part of this one. In fact, I wasn't sure what dead meant and wasn't prepared for what came next.

Death, laying rooms, cemeteries, and burial is not for a youngin'. Especially a youngin' who has a vivid imagination.

I made the mistake of wanting to go with Ma to sit with Jennie. Shoot, I didn't even know the meaning of "sit." I thought Ma was going to visit Grammaw and Grampaw. We took off in the buggy after our evening meal. Ma was unusually quiet as she wheeled the buggy to a stop at the base of the winding path below Grammaw's house. The old road leading to Grampaw and Grammaw's house was unusually steep, and Ma didn't want to take the chance of leading the horses up it at night. Ma stepped down from the buggy, took the coal oil lantern from the loop, lit the wick and placed the lantern on the ground. She gently lifted me from the seat and told me to carry the lantern very carefully while she struggled with a basket of food.

We began walking up the winding path. With every step we took, the shaky lantern would cast an eerie glow to the ground. Halfway up the path, a big man stepped out of the shadows, scooped the basket out of Ma's arms, and at the same time hefted me onto his shoulders. I straddled his neck with my legs and held on to his head. Ma took the lantern from me and walked in front of us, lighting the pathway with the lantern. We reached the house in a very short time.

The house looked strange. The front porch had lanterns all along the perimeter. The front door was ajar. I was beginning to think, "I should have stayed with Pa." Stepping onto the front porch, I took a peek inside the door. Goosebumps covered my entire body, and I began to scratch. My first instinct was to turn around and run as fast as my little legs could run, but my brain shut down and my feet wouldn't move.

It was dark in there. Pitch black dark! I could see a big long box draped in material and a rocking chair beside the box. Those things sure didn't look familiar to me. Not the loving things I pictured in my mind. I heard Ma tell the man to head on home. We would be there for the night.

"Th' night? Th' whole night! Does she actually think I'm goin' in thar?" I tried to scream. Nothing came out of my mouth. A big wad of air was closing up my breathing tube and nothing would come out. Ma took my hand, and we started in the front door. My heart was pounding so hard I could feel it in my ears. As we approached the big box, I could smell sweet perfume. It smelled like lavender, lots of lavender, and it was making me sick as a goat. Not only that but my insides were becoming shakier than a hula skirt.

Ma said, "J. D., I want'cha ta see sumthin'." She lifted me up toward the big box and said, "Jennie's a'sleepin'un we're goin' ta spend th' nite with her so Grammaw and Grampaw can get sum rest. Thay've been awake fer sum time now un we have ta help'em.

"Besides," Ma continued, "Grammaw has ta wake up every few hours ta tend lil' baby Jo. Thet lil' baby needs her nourishment ta survive. Maybe Grammaw will let'cha help feed'er. J. D., ya need ta be a real good friend ta Tut. Thet little boy is a grievin' fer his Ma un needs all th' love we can give'm. Iffen ya do thet, one'o these days, ya will get th' golden stars in yer crown."

I said, "But Ma, iffen she's asleep why do we have ta stay here? Cain't she sleep by herself? When she wakes up she can feed th' baby. I wanna go home!"

Ma firmly said, "No! Someone needs ta be with her till she goes ta th' cemetery. Hush, now, we don't want ta wake lil' baby Jo."

Cemetery? I didn't like that word. If the cemetery was as bad as it sounded, why were we going? Ma settled down in the rocking chair and began to hum. She placed a blanket on the floor, gave me a feather pillow and told me to go to sleep. I'm not certain when I finally fell asleep. The last thing I remembered was Ma stroking my hair and the gentle soothing hum of her beautiful voice.

The morning came, and the house was filled with people. Hill folk came from miles around. I didn't know there were so many people scattered in the hills. Some of the lady folk were crying, wiping their tears with lacy handkerchiefs and hugging Grammaw and Grampaw. A few of them told of their grief and how they coped without their loved ones. Everyone had a story to tell. All the stories were alike but different in a strange sort of way.

A kindly old gentleman took Grampaw aside. They began to converse about Jennie, when she was born, how old she was when she passed away and who were the surviving kinfolk. The old gentleman asked Grampaw if he had a family Bible. The Bible was a family's best source of information, and these words about Jennie needed to be written down. It was God's word in the Bible which sustained a body in need of comfort and was a written reminder of those who went to their reward. This way they would always be in mind and close to God.

Pa, Effie Mae, Aunt Sukie and Tut came to the house all decked out in the finest clothes they had. Pa had put some of my clothes on Tut. They fit him right nice. Pa handed Ma her clean dress, then took me aside to change my clothes and comb my hair. By the time I got ready, everyone was waiting outside.

Big, burly, strapping men carried the big box with Jennie inside and placed her on a flat hay wagon. Grammaw and Grampaw climbed aboard. We all proceeded to walk behind the wagon. The horses hooves plodding the ground was the only sound heard. No one was talking. Silence! Silence! Even the birds seemed to be in reverence.

We crossed over a small ridge behind the house. Coming upon a partial clearing, I could see rocks standing on end. Some were carved with names while others had dried flowers scattered about. Grampaw gently stopped the wagon beneath a large mulberry tree. The same men took the box, placed a rope under the base of the coffin and lowered it into a freshly dug hole. We all stood round the edge of the hole, tossing clumps of dirt upon the top of the coffin, saying, "Ashes to ashes, dust to dust." One of the men began to speak of Jennie, of how she loved picking the mulberries from this particular tree she planted, then we recited Bible verses and sang two songs,

"Shall We Gather At the River" and "When We Hear Those Golden Bells for You and Me."

At this point in time, I think I might have actually realized what death, laying rooms and cemeteries were about. Death is final. Laying rooms mean respect. Cemeteries, the peaceful sleep provider.

Jennie was gone, but her legacy of love for Tut and lil' baby Jo was just beginning.

The Secret of Frog Holler

Frog Holler was the prettiest place in the daylight but the scariest, spookiest and noisiest frog-croaking, cricket-chirping, snake-slithering creek and woodland you could find at nighttime.

Frog Holler was one of two hollers in our neck of the woods. The other one was Hoot Holler. A holler is what we called a hole in the hills. The hole stops at the base of the hill and when you holler at someone, your voice carries and bounces off whatever get in its way. Sort of like an echo. Hollers, for some people, were not the most desirable place to live, but we had the most wonderful childhood and upbringing anyone could ever want.

Anyway, Frog Holler was at the west of our house. Frog Holler Bayou ran west to east and split when it came to Hoot Holler, which was on the east side of our house. We never seemed to be in danger of rising water from the creek behind our house because the northern part of our land dropped at least one hundred feet straight down into a ravine. All rain seemed to gravitate to the ravine and swirl into eddies like small snow-capped mountains. It was a beautiful sight when the water flowed gently down the slopes but very dangerous when the spring rains began to pour from the heavens.

The Hoot Holler side had the best swimming hole a body could ever jump into, let alone swing from a vine over and pretend you had wings, but the Frog Holler side was another story. Later on, I'll tell you about Hoot Holler.

During the day, Frog Holler was as peaceful and graceful as birds in flight. The massive old oak and elm trees had been standing for many years, with their arching branches dangling toward the ground, ivy entangled throughout most of the tree limbs. Sunlight would flicker through the leaves to cast shadows on green mossy rocks and decaying residue of leaves from many years of seasonal changes. Because the holler was on the west side of our house, very little sunlight managed to infiltrate the mass of flora that seemed to creep up from nowhere. At night, I'm telling you, it's creepier than goose bumps on an old bald head, and nobody would venture off in that neck of the woods even if someone yelled, "Thar's gold in them thar hills."

One night Pa set out to look for one of our cows who had dropped her calf during the birthing season. Pa figured she had wandered into the cool shade of one of the oak trees near the edge of the holler to give birth and was either lost or tangled up in the underbrush. Old Brown Bertha had been one of our best milk cows, and Pa wasn't going to let her lay hurt or get eaten by some of the critters which roamed the night in search of old rotten carcasses.

Not long after Pa left the house, the noises began to creep from the holler in search of anything that was within earshot. The frogs would greedeep and cherclok with massive throats billowing with every croak. Pretty soon screeches and moans would echo with resounding bangs and thuds. These sounds would continue all night long, and I don't mind telling you, it was a mite hard to fall asleep. I was in fear that whatever making all the noises would come slithering through our old front door and consume all of us. Ma would say, "Not to worrie, th' sounds'll be gone come daybreak. Don't forgit ta say yer prayers and remember th' sounds won't be thar tomorrow night."

Somehow Ma was always right. The noises were there just about every other night. But tonight I was worried about Pa. It had been a great while since he left the house to find Old

Brown Bertha and her calf. My mind was racing in fear for Pa, but before I could say anything to Ma, Pa came bouncing through the door saying he had found old Bertha and her baby calf and had already put them in the barn for safekeeping.

Something was a mite strange with Pa. I heard him tell Ma, "It's doin' jist fine un shore is good." I reckoned he was talking about the baby calf, but in the back of my mind, I was sure Pa was up to something. He was just a little too bouncy and full of the impish looks. Not to worry: I planned to talk Tut into going into Frog Holler with me the very next day. I figured there was more to Frog Holler than met the eye or the ear.

After I got most of my chores finished, I asked Pa if I could go find Tut and take a quick swim to cool off. I promised to finish whatever needed to be done when I came home. Pa sure was in a good mood. He didn't put up a howl and told me to go have fun.

I trekked across the open field and headed toward Tut's house. Tut lived about a mile away from our house, near Millers Crossin. Millers Crossin wasn't much to look at, though. It had a deserted old wood mill, a general store built almost inside a hill, an old unused train stop for water and caves. Big caves! Crossing the railroad tracks dividing our property, I had to jump a lot of big ditches and climb a hill before I could walk on solid ground to yell for Tut.

Everybody seemed to be in such great spirits. Grammaw Ellison said, "Why shore, Honey, ye youngins go have sum fun. No sense in werkin' all yer life."

Tut and I just looked at each other in disbelief. When I explained to Tut where we were going and what we were going to do, he said, "NO! I ain't goin' ta set foot in Frog Holler. Ya know how many times we've been told ta stay out of thet holler and whut will happen ta both of us iffen we don't mind yore Pa and my Grammaw. If somethin' doesn't git us in th' holler, we'll be hollerin' when thay're through beatin' our backsides."

Somehow as usual, I managed to talk Tut into poking our noses where they didn't belong.

Since Pa thought we were going swimming and Grammaw Ellison thought we were going to my house, we were home free. Or so we thought! We sneaked back across the open field and headed toward Frog Holler. We ran so fast that our feet didn't even touch the ground.

At last we were at the base of Frog Holler. It wasn't very spooky but sure was dark and dank. We made our way through the ivy-covered trees, over boulders slicker than greasy wheel spokes, and slid down several gullies, and we landed square dab into the biggest mess of sluice holes we ever thought of slopping through. It looked like our old sow's wallowing hole. Not only that, leeches were stuck to us like stick tight weeds. Both of us were red with welts from our heads to our toes, and itched to death from what might have been a poison ivy vine which we used to free ourselves from the mud hole. We were in one fine mess, all because of my hankering to see what went on in the holler at night.

After we removed all the blood-sucking leaches, we found a waterfall big enough to wash off all the mud and yuck from our bodies. I decided to tell Tut that we'd better forget about this adventure and head on home when Tut slammed his hand over my mouth and pointed toward some kind of weird-looking contraption sticking out between two big boulders.

We inched our way very slowly and quietly toward this thing. It was burping and gurgling like nothing we had ever heard. There were big old jugs turned upside down and the "jugs" were like Pa and Grammaw Ellison's cure-all medicine. Medicine, we were told, "only belonged to big folk." Firewood was piled in big stacks and the embers under the old black belly, makeshift stove were smoldering. Funny thing about that stove! The flue was pointed toward the ground and no smoke was coming out. A long curled pipe was dripping liquid into an old barrel as steam escaped into the atmosphere. There wasn't an odor, except for the mounds of moldy old corn and the remains of burned wood.

Because we were thirsty, Tut grabbed up an old gourd drinking cup and swigged down a big gulp of the drippings. He looked at me, expressionless, for a long time. His face turned a bright shade of red, his eyeballs bulged out, and the hair on the back of his neck stuck straight out. He gasped for air, grabbed his throat and his tongue flew out of his mouth. He was whistling through his teeth and tried to talk. All he could say was "Arrrrrrk!"

I couldn't let Tut outdo me, so I took the gourd and scooped it into the drippings. I gulped down the juice just a little too fast. All I can remember is my mouth being set on fire as though I had just eaten the whole dad blamed fireplace, legs going all limp, and slumping like runny jelly to the ground. Tut was leaning over me saying, "J.D. er, er, er ye daid?" Tut was banging me on the head and pounding my back so hard, my teeth rattled like a rattlesnake about to strike.

After I regained my composure and the trees stopped swaying, I stupidly grabbed that dirty old gourd and swigged down another gulp. Before long, me and Tut were pretty zonked. We realized we had found a still! We had overheard Pa and Grampaw talking about stills and good tasting "corn likker" but never knew one was so close. We also heard about men who would shoot a body, if they had a mind to, especially if anyone dared set foot on their cooking grounds. Cooking grounds were off limits to anyone not invited. Especially a revenuer and nosy kids who didn't have enough sense to come in out of a driving rain storm! Now we knew why we had been to told to "stay outta thet holler." We found a real moonshine, white lightenin', huffing and puffing, "corn likker" still. We began giggling. We were so giddy that if I hadn't known better, I would have thought we were girls!

Everything began to look funny and we sounded goofy. We couldn't talk clearly, things seemed to be moving back and forth and our feet wouldn't stay on the ground. Our feet had a mind of their own! We were swaying back and forth watching everything turn into a massive blob of blur and multiply with great vigor. I grabbed at Tut and told him to quit moving cause there were just too many green-eyed Tuts standing around me.

Then we got sick. When I say sick…I mean SICK!

I finally managed to sit down on a big boulder and could feel my stomach curdling. I looked at Tut who had perched his rear end between two rocks. His eyes were green and the outline of his lips was white. Each time we looked at each other, we'd heave and that made us sicker. The smell alone was adding to the way we felt. We cupped our hands over the tops of our heads, hoping to hold down the pain that was shooting out our ears. Our heads were pounding with the force of a sledgehammer, our queasy stomachs were dancing a two step and we had a powerful stink flung on us!

All of a sudden we heard two men talking. They were coming up a hill toward the still. Tut and I managed to crawled behind the big boulders and quietly watched as they approached the dripping elixir. The men were very large with barrel chests, long, lanky legs and arms to match. Their long hair, sticking out from under well-worn hats, hadn't been cut in a very long time. Each of them was carrying double-barreled shotguns, and we knew immediately to give them a wide berth. They picked up one jug at a time, funneling them with the clear cooked brew, and carefully sealed them with a piece of flour sack and string. They piled the jugs neatly in rows and marked them with a big X. One of the men piled logs near the stove while the other one shoveled old, smelly ground corn and cobs into a big kettle and covered it tightly with a slab of metal. They began to say how they'd come back tomorrow night and get the fire started for this batch to cook. "Cain't let this stuff cook in th' daylight. Thar's jist too much smoke! Don't want nobody pokin' up 'round here messin' up our doins."

When they left, Tut and I did the same. We followed them quietly down a well-worn path as they covered every few feet with old dead branches and underbrush. We finally made it out of the woods, only to find the path leading right past our house where Pa found old Brown Bertha and her calf.

We didn't realize how long we had been gone. Ma was yelling at the top of her lungs for us. "Whar have ye been? I been a hollerin' fer nigh on ta an hour fer ya ta git on home. We done et'er vittles. Ya best git on ta th' house afore yer vittles tarn ta hard tack. Iffen ya boys don't take heed ta whut I be a sayin, frum now on, ye can eat with th' hawgs!"

Tut and I looked at each other. That sick feeling crept up into our throats. Vittles? The last thing we wanted was vittles! We reluctantly sat down and ate. Tut said he'd best be going home before it got too dark. He thanked Ma for the good vittles and set out for home.

That night while lying in bed, I found myself at peace with the eerie noises emanating from Frog Holler every other night. We knew the reason for Pa and Grammaw Ellison's jovial condition, and Tut and I had two major finds...a place to test the "medicine" and the secret of Frog Holler.

Hoot Holler Kids

We were called the Hoot Holler Kids. I guess we were called that because we liked to hunt for hoot owls. Those critters were a mite mean bunch if they were cornered, but shucks, we weren't afraid of them. What could a stupid bird do?

We wanted to find out really bad if their heads would turn all the way around backwards, like Pa said. We were always being joke-poked and laughed at 'cause we were so gullible. We figured if Pa said it, it had to be gospel and didn't pay any mind to the fun pokin'. Besides, we knew in our hearts and minds that we could prove it. We were going to catch one of those critters and lay claim to fame. We would prove we weren't afraid of the dark or anything that went bump in the night. We knew we were right and planned on catching a hooter before the sun came up in the morning.

My sister Effie Mae and I plotted how we would sneak out of the house and trek off to the woods. We didn't tell Aunt Sukie 'cause she made too much noise and was too fussy. When the sun slid down among the pines and the critters started to take over the night with howling and prowling and Ma and Pa were fast asleep, we'd nab a "hooter."

I sneaked into Pa and Ma's room and sure enough, Pa was rattling the rafters with loud snoring and Ma was shuffling back and forth trying to find a spot suitable for her backside, sort of like an old hound dog trying to scratch a spot in the dirt to get cool. Effie Mae grabbed the old coal oil lantern and we headed for the woods.

We figured it wouldn't take more than an hour or two to prove our point. We were wrong! Those dumb old "hooters" must have seen us coming. We were gone for almost all the dark hours and were skunked by those "hooters." We had just gone to bed when Ma yelled for us youngins' to get out of the bed.

"Thar's werk ta do," she hollered.

Pa said, "J.D., go slop th' hawgs."

Pa knew I wasn't too fond of those smelly old "rooters," and besides, that old sow was always chasing me 'cause I was always picking up her little piglets. But today I was going to whomp the daylights out of her if she looked at me crossways. My eyeballs looked and felt like two watering holes in a pile of sand and I was plum tuckered out from not getting any sleep. Ma and Pa must have known what Effie Mae and I had been doing 'cause we were dragging around like worn-out shoes.

Effie Mae and Aunt Sukie, my other dumb old sister, were scrubbing our wearing clothes on a scrub board. Effie Mae was stumbling all over the place and dropping the clean scrubbed clothes in the dirt. I saw Ma and Pa winking at one another and snickering 'cause they knew we had been up to something. We scooted around trying to get our chores done with one eye open and the other one shut. We tried to sneak away to get some shut-eye but Pa would yell, "Jist one more thang, J.D., jist one more thang." Those "thangs" were a killin' me.

Before the day was over, my best friend Tut dropped by to see if I had a mind to go fishing. Since I was dragging and the chores were lagging, Pa set us both straight. NO fishing! Pa told Tut to get on home and help Grampaw. Without saying a word, Tut looked at me with a questioning look: "Did ya git thet 'hooter?'" I shrugged my shoulders and shook my head no. I told Tut to come back that evening and spend the night. We'd camp out on the front porch, maybe catch some fireflies. Yup! Tut knew what I meant.

The day seemed to drag on forever. I thought it would never get dark outside and everyone would stay up longer than usual, but finally Pa said it was time to batten down the hatches. At last, everyone would be asleep. Everyone but us! I could hardly wait. I was so tired from all the chores and desperate for sleep, but come you know where or high water, we were going to catch a "hooter."

We sneaked off the front porch and headed for the woods. Not far into the woods was the biggest old "hooter" we had ever laid eyes on. Tut and I had to figure out a way to get that hooter out of the tree. While Tut waited on me and kept an eye on the hooter, I ran as fast as I could back to our old shed, grabbed up a gunny sack, a piece of long wrapping cord, an old chicken head that Ma had buried in the postin' pile and one of her butcher knives. I ran back to the woods so fast that my heart felt as though it would pound right out of the top of my head. I fell on the ground and finally caught my breath of air. The hooter was still perched in the tree. We could barely see the hooter, but we knew the hooter could see us. We tied the strapping cord around the chicken head and flung it into the air. Nothing! Tut decided to tie a big old rock on the other end of the cord and give it another fling.

Big mistake. It went into the air, twisted around and konked me square dab on my noggin, knocking me onto the ground. The top of my forehead began swelling until I had a goose egg the size of Aunt Lillie's backside. With all the confusion, old hooter flew into another tree and looked at us like we were both stupid. After Tut and I had a go-around with each other, our tempers cooled and we gave the chicken head another toss. This time the rock flew through the air with great precision and wrapped itself around a tree limb with the chicken head dangling about one foot off the ground. It was just a matter of time. All we had to do was wait and wait and wait. Pretty soon the wind began moving the chicken head back and forth like a little mouse scurrying on the ground.

At last old hooter took the bait. Hooter swooped down with

his claws and hooked the chicken head. The cord wrapped around one of his feet and we rushed in with the gunnysack. Tut went for the hooter and the hooter went for him. The hooter's claws came nigh on to jerking the hair right out of Tut's head. Tut was screaming bloody murder and flinging the gunny sack in the air. I knew if Tut kept on screaming, flailing the air and kissing the ground, we could kiss that old hooter goodbye.

I tackled Tut and clamped my hand over his mouth to keep him from screaming. We had another go-around with each other and realized the hooter was still hanging by the cord and his wings were flapping so hard the leaves on the ground were kicking up a dust. We grabbed up the gunny sack and started cramming the hooter head first into it trying to keep the hooter from gouging his claws into our skin. Tut finally got the hooter inside the gunnysack and I wrapped the cord around the top. I managed to cut the cord with the butcher knife I sneaked from Ma's kitchen. We had our "hooter"!

Since it was getting awfully close to daybreak, we decided to take the hooter home and examine his head come daylight. We trekked back to the house with the hooter in the gunnysack and poked him in an old covered box near the woodshed that Pa'd built for Ma for the kindling wood. We figured to examine old hooter's head before Ma or Pa could find out what we had been up to in the middle of the night. Tweren't to be the way we figured!

You might have known. Pa woke up early to begin the day's chores and headed straight for the woodshed. I heard Pa tell Ma that he would bring in some kindling for the cookstove so she could get the biscuits rising for breakfast.

Well now, I'm here to tell you that Pa let out a scream that would raise the hair on the back of your neck. Pa found our hooter or the hooter found him. Pa kept yelling, "Ma, git th' butcher knife, git th' butcher knife. Ma, git th' butcher knife.

Now Ma now!" That hooter's claws had latched into Pa's arm and into his lower lip. They were looking straight way into each other's eyes. Shucks, I didn't know that Ma could run so fast. She shot out the door like buckshot from a shotgun with the butcher knife in one hand and the old green medicine in the other. Effie Mae and Aunt Sukie came running 'cause they were scared, and Tut and I came running because we knew if Ma chopped off the hooter's head we'd never find out if the hooters head sure enough turned all the way around.

Because we lived so far up in the hills, the only doctor we ever saw had left some old green puke medicine he said would "knock someone out" if anyone got hurt real bad. Well, Pa needed this green puke medicine, but I figured the poor old hooter needed it more than Pa did. When I got to the shed, Pa was sitting on the chopping stump a bleeding right bad, and the hooter was flapping his wings. They were a mess. I stuck a rag with the green puke medicine into Pa's face and both Pa and the hooter konked out. We loosened the claws from Pa's arm and lip and sneaked the hooter into an empty chicken coop so we could check its head before Pa could turn it loose or make "hooter" hash out of it.

Well, I suckered us into more dad blamed work. While Pa was laid up for a spell, Effie Mae, Aunt Sukie, Tut and I had to double up on the chores. Effie Mae and Aunt Sukie had to do Ma's work while she was tending Pa. Tut and I were elected to slop the hogs, chop the wood, pile up rocks for a wall and any cockeyed thing Pa could think up while he was sitting in his rocking chair. Both of them were on vacation sipping mint water while the sweat was pouring off all us kids.

Effie Mae and Aunt Sukie were mad at me for getting them in trouble with Ma. Ma was ticked off at me and Tut for bringing that critter home, and Pa was mad as old billy ned because I stuck the green puke medicine up his nose, making him fall off the chopping stump. Well shoot, I didn't know he would bonk his head on a rock, and for sure didn't know the hooter was going to make his lip look like a fat old toad.

The only one who wasn't in trouble was the hooter.

I was all tuckered out from all the added chores and having to dodge all the spitfire, madder-than-wet-hen females. If that hooter knew what was good for him, his dumb old head had better turn all the way around. 'Cause if it didn't turn all the way 'round, I was fixin' to twist it off.

Now, if you plan on catching a hooter, forget it! I'm living proof and telling you right now, those tales I thought was gospel from Pa just ain't rightly so. Because of the nature of wild things, I found out right quick what nature is all about.

Heads don't turn all the way around, claws have a powerful way of making you screech, wings jab the daylights out of your eyeballs and the feathers snuff out the breath that pumps up your lungs. Yes siree, that hooter taught me a lesson. Just because somebody says something may be right, it doesn't necessitate dying to find out.

Besides, that hooter got away!

Ya Gotta Swim Or Die

The general store and the depot were the only two stopping places at the Crossin except for a couple of lean shacks, which the railroad people owned. Most people living in the hollers were content with what they had. We helped each other saw the felled trees into wood planks for building and divided up the harvested grain seed for winter. Everybody pitched in to help a body if they were in trouble or got together just for the fun of being together.

Pa would say, "Th wurld is a changin' a mite too fast. Them auttiemobiles create a powerful dust bowl. Why, afore ye know it, th' cittie folk'll be square dab in th' Crossin."

Pa was sorely right. Mr. Matlock's general store was the only store for miles around in the hills, and most folk would bring part of their crops to the store for him to sell. A lot of the city folk who had money to buy the fancy automobiles would venture to our neck of the woods just to see the countryside or to buy the fresh produce at the general store.

The Crossin wasn't much to look at, but for us, it was one of the best places in the world. We had a powerful good time playing around the general store. Every now and then, Mr. Matlock would give us licorice sticks if we helped him move big baskets of goods from one side to the other side of the store. It didn't make too much sense moving it all the time, but if he wanted to give away candy, we'd be happy to move anything.

The shelves at the general store housed cookie jars chock full of licorice, chewing gum, stinking, foul-tasting horehound sticks, peppermint and cinnamon chews and pickles! Mr. Matlock would reach into the pickle jar and pull out the biggest old pickles that dripped with the sourest brine and made our jaws pop and crackle with spit. Boy they were good. Anyone who ever ate one of those pickles sure knew right away where lockjaw got its name.

All of us—Aunt Sukie, Effie Mae, Tut and I—would wait for Ma to finish her shopping. Ma only shopped for things she couldn't grow, like flour, sugar and some staples necessary for cooking. We didn't have a lot of money, so Ma would sew clothes, aprons and potholders for Mr. Matlock to sell to the city folk. She'd say, "It ain't much but every little bit helps us, one way or athuther." Ma was a good woman, full of love for everything and all of God's children.

After we helped Ma unload the cooking stuff from the wagon, she'd say, "Now you youngins git! Go on un play fer a spell, but be shore ta git home afore Pa commences ta yell fer ye." We knew if Pa had to yell more than a couple of times, we were out of earshot and in a big heap of trouble. We all started down the viney path, and I was thinking about the fresh water and how it would feel jumping into Miller Creek. It was so hot outside and the cool, clear water would soon soothe the flesh.

Tut was walking behind me and mumbling about not wanting to go swimming. Aunt Sukie and Effie Mae were running ahead of me screaming, "Last one in is a rotten aigg." I had never actually seen Tut swim cause he always kicked the water, saying the water made his ears hurt if they got wet. "I'll set this one out," Tut would say. Well, not today!

Tut was bigger than me and always thought he was older, but he was wrong. That boy was about my age and lankier than a bullwhip. It always seemed that his legs were trying to catch up with his body when he walked, and his arms didn't know what his brain was doing. His brain would think one thing and his arms would do another. It was like he was on "hold" or stuck out in a tree somewhere. Tut would stutter when he became nervous and would say, " J.J.J. D., I, I, I don't fffeel like swis, swis, swimming. My ee ears are hur, hurting."

Everybody except Tut had jumped into the water. We were swinging from the Muskedine vine, dropping into the water making big splashes and waves. We looked at one another in wonderment as to why Tut hadn't even wet his toes. Effie Mae yelled for Tut to jump in: " Ma won't git mad iffen you git yore clothes wet un neither will Grammaw. Thay know we're swimmin'." Well, Tut picked himself off the ground and began running real fast toward the water. When Tut hit the water the splash almost got the Crossin wet. After the water stopped waving and rippling, we wiped the water out of our eyes but Tut was nowhere in site. We didn't think too much about it because we thought Tut was swimming under water getting ready to spook Effie Mae or Aunt Sukie.

Effie Mae ducked under the water to check on Tut. All of a sudden, Effie Mae came to the surface yelling for us to get help for Tut. Effie Mae flung a scare on Aunt Sukie and me. We ducked under the water in a panic. There was Tut. That goofball hadn't cracked his head open or got caught between rocks. He was holding on to a rock under the water. His arms were squeezing a rock like leaches on a leg and his eyeballs were blinking real fast. His jaws were blown up with air like a toad trying to get away from a bird. We couldn't pry him loose for nothin' and we were getting disgusted with not being able to breathe. Effie Mae looked so funny under water. Her long legs were stretched out, pushing against a rock and pulling Tut with her arms. They both looked like suction cups or somewhat like an octopus.

In the confusion, Aunt Sukie swam back to the bank, then back toward Tut. All of a sudden, Tut came loose from the rock and shot straight up in the air. Effie Mae was doing somersaults under the water and Tut was yelling at the top of his lungs about a snake biting him. Aunt Sukie tied the muscadine vine around his waist and we pulled him out of the water.

We got Tut on the creek bank and tried to get him to shut his mouth and sit those bony, shaky legs down. He was driving us nuts. He wouldn't shut up or sit down! All he could do was say, "Sn, sn, sn, snake." I threatened to heave him back into the water when Aunt Sukie began laughing so hard, tears streamed down her cheeks. Effie Mae was getting real mad 'cause Tut nearly drowned the two of them. She ran as fast as she could and tackled Tut square dab in the middle of his gut and slammed his face in the mud. He quit saying, "Sn, sn, sn, snake," when his kisser hit the ground. Effie Mae flung a punch at Aunt Sukie, but before she could punch her lights out, I spied a funny-looking thing sticking out of Tut's behind.

Aunt Sukie had stuck Tut in the behind with a great big thorn to get him to turn loose of the rock. That thorn was Tut's "Sn, sn, snake!" Tut sure enough wasn't going to sit for any length of time so he might as well learn to swim. Well, before the day was over, Tut purt near drowned us all but sure enough learned how to swim. In the hills, you've gotta swim or die!

The Outhouse

The outhouse wasn't anyone's favorite place to visit, but let's face it, we all had to go one time or another! Sometimes it was more than usual, especially when you've eaten too many persimmons or guzzled down too many swigs of apple cider.

Our outhouse was about one hundred feet west from the house, toward Frog Holler. That doesn't seem too far away until a body gets to running and tries to beat whatever is defeating the purpose. It seems as though whatever lurked inside the outhouse wasn't nearly as bad as what lurked inside the body.

One day when Tut and I were feeling a mite ornery and bent on creating a bit of mischief, we decided to spook anyone who happened to be in dire need of the premises. We took to the woods to talk about our little scheme. Sitting down on the ground, we drew pictures in the dirt of our impending devious act and rolled with laughter as to how our unsuspecting prey would react.

Our outhouse was a two-holer. Pa built the outhouse with two people in mind. A body who was in a major hurry wouldn't have to wait for their turn. The compartments weren't very large but large enough to accommodate a sit-down and space for an old Sears catalog and soaked corn shucks or corncobs. Ma would soak the corn shucks and cobs and stick them in a bucket. The shucks and cobs were okay, sometimes, if you remembered to squeeze 'em out. If you didn't squeeze 'em, it was a mess! A Sears catalog was known as a "wish" book. While sitting on the throne, you could thumb through the pages and wish for everything, knowing full well those wishes may never come true. However, each page had the destiny of being used for toilet paper.

Several times, Aunt Sukie or Effie Mae would holler their heads off, saying, "You used th' page I wanted ta look at." Shucks, they were lucky. More than once I'd grab up a shuck or cob that hadn't been soaked, and rue the day because of the itch it created. Pa would say, "J. D., yer sisters' have delicate skin un it won't hurt ya ta save th' catalog pages fer'em." Delicate skin my foot! Those dad blamed females had Pa buffaloed.

After Tut and I figured how to work our little scheme, we meandered back to the house snickering with every breath. We knew one of the girls, if not both of them, would need the use of the outhouse in a matter of hours. They would always wait till Ma, Pa or I had been because Pa would kill any spiders or creepy crawlers which perched in the rafters above our heads. Effie Mae and Aunt Sukie didn't like crawly little bugs, especially those kind which had the propensity to bite. They were just too dad blamed fussy for their own good.

Because it was getting close to noon, Pa had several more chores to do before we could sit down to eat our noon meal or even think about our little plotted scheme. Pa requested immediate help in the smokehouse. It wouldn't have been very smart, especially to our backsides, to defy his request, so Tut and I began helping Pa. It smelled right good in the smokehouse. Pa was preparing the smokehouse 'cause it was almost the season to butcher a hog. Pa needed all the help he could muster. Knives needed sharpening, hay had to be placed under the butchering table, grappling hooks needed cleaning, and big kegs were positioned for fat renderings.

Pa never butchered until the fall and winter season because it was too hot in the summer to keep the meat fresh. While the hickory smoke permeated the meat, the cold winter air and snow would stable and preserve the meat. Pa would then salt them down for added protection and wrap the shanks in burlap. Big hooks would hold them off the ground by suspending them in mid-air to prevent any critter from snatching a meal or two. More times than I can count on my hands and feet foxes ventured out of the hills in search of food and were successful in sneaking off with one of Pa's hams. Anyway, we helped Pa finish up the chores and went about fulfilling our little scheme.

The first step was snatching a string of thread. Ma always had plenty of crochet thread for tatting our pillowcases. Since the thread came on rolls of cardboard, Tut had to find the scissors. In the process of cutting the thread, Tut placed the scissors back in the sewing box upside down so that the lid didn't shut properly. First mistake!

While Tut was getting the thread, I was searching for the largest tarantula I could find. Tarantulas are the ugliest, hairiest, creepiest bug-eyed spiders imaginable, but are non-poisonous. I didn't want to hurt the girls; I just wanted to scare the daylights out of them. Tut and I turned over every rock, stirred up rotten leaves and rolled over dead tree limbs before we found our tarantula. He was a big one! Tut held the tarantula down with a stick while I slid the thread under his massive hairy body. His legs were sticky and kept pushing the thread away. The tarantula jumped toward Tut and landed square dab on Tut's arm. Tut stood up, turned around in circles, stomped the ground, flailed his arms in a panic and the tarantula flew ten feet in the air. "I ha, ha, ha, hate them thangs, J. D.! Thay give me th' wi, wi, willies," Tut screamed. It took me ten minutes to find that tarantula after Tut did his little screaming fit. After I cornered the tarantula, I made Tut wrap the thread around the body while I held the spider by its back. Finally Mr. Tarantula was prepared to go to work.

We sneaked to the outhouse. Tut climbed on the roof while I went in the ladies' side. I pushed the loose end of the thread up through a crack in the ceiling and Tut tied a stick on the other end. Mr. Tarantula was dangling at just the right height. When Effie Mae or Aunt Sukie sat down, Mr. Tarantula would barely touch the tops of their heads. Just enough, slightly arousing the skin to create goose bumps. Tut leaped from the roof and we disappeared behind the barn to watch.

Sure enough the girls came sauntering toward the outhouse. Both of them went inside. Tut and I didn't hear a peep. Not a scream, nothing! They came out just like they went in. Giggling, with not a care in the world. Tut and I looked at each other in bewilderment.

"Whut happened, J. D.? Thay didn't scream one nary little bit."

"Dang it, Tut, I don't know. Are ya sure ya tied a stick on th' other end of th' thread ta keep it frum fallin' threw th' kraks?"

"It wus a hangin' frum th' ceiling, wudden't it?" Tut snorted back.

"Well, thet tarantula is somewhar in thar, and we best find it afore Ma comes out here or we'us goin' ta be in a heap a trouble," I snapped. We crept back in the outhouse in search of the spider. We never found the thing. Deciding it crawled out the door, we went about our business.

Several hours later, having eaten a bunch of apples, Tut and I needed to use the outhouse. Tut was in a hurry and rushed in the boys' side of the house. I waited for him beside the door, talking through the cracks waiting for my turn. All of a sudden, Tut came screeching out the door, his pant legs pushed down toward his ankles, tripped over his feet and went crashing to the ground. His rear end was jutting in the air while his mouth was full of dirt and grass.

"J. D., it's thet da, da, da, danged spi, spi, spider. It was hung up in my hair!" screeched Tut.

"Tut, yore loco. Ain't no way thet spider could be a hangin' on our side of th' outhouse."

"Go see fer yourself," Tut sputtered.

I went inside and couldn't find that spider. Deciding the urge was necessary, I sat down to relieve myself of too many apples. After completing my task, I used the ever-present corncobs to erase my backside. I gathered my composure, and Tut and I went back toward the house. Halfway there I began to itch. Not just a little itch. It was a full-blown, scoot on your backside itch! Pretty soon, I was scratching so hard I couldn't see straight. My hands were itching so bad I had to shove them in my pockets. What in the world was the matter with me? Running toward the house, I yelled for Ma. "Ma, sumpthins' makin' me itch real bad," I said in a panic.

"Well, go find yer Pa un have him take a look see," she replied with a sneaky grin.

I cornered Pa in the barn with my plight. He took one look at my backside and began to laugh. "It's pisin ivy, J.D. Ya done sat yore butt down inna mess a pisin ivy!"

"But Pa," I said, "I didn't sit down in no pisin ivy. I didn't start ta itch till I used th' corn shucks."

"Whar's Tut?" Pa questioned.

"He tuk off toards home. He was feelin' a mite porely. His gut was a hurtin' un his hair wus stickin' upright. He wus a mess, Pa!" I replied.

Pa said, "How'd Tut like th' spider?"

"How'd ya know 'bout th' spider?" I sheepishly asked.

"Well, I wus in th' tuther side of th' outhouse when you an Tut were hangin' th' spider. I heard everthang ya said and knowed you and Tut needed ta be larned a lesson. I took th' spider down and hung it in th' boys side. Knowin' th' two of you and yer glut fer apples, it twudn't be long afore one of you'ens got a taste of yer own medicine," Pa stated. In fact, he said, "I told yer Ma whut you and Tut were a doin'."

Walking back to the house, Pa gave me a lecture on why I should treat the girls more gently. "Ya see, son, girls'er special. Thay don't contrive devious thangs. It's jist not in thar nature.

Thay're supposed ta be frilly and fussy. Thay wouldn't think o' bein' nasty er pullin' double dog tricks." Those words slid off his tongue with pride. I was just about to swear off any more tricks when Effie Mae and Aunt Sukie began to taunt me with a sinister hiss.

"How'd'ja like th' corn shucks, J. D.? Was it soft un nice er was it itchy like pisin ivy? Na, na, na, na, na, na, J. D.'s got an itch, he got it frum th' corn shucks, th' corn shucks did th' trick. We rubbed 'em in th' ivy patch, them itchy viney leaves, th' kind thet makes ya itch like mad and now ya cain't sit down. Na, na, na, na, na, na, J.D.'s got th' itch, he looks jist like a stupid clown, a clown which cain't sit down! Na, na, na, na, na, na, J. D,'s got th' itch, he got it frum th' corn shucks, th' corn shucks did th' trick." Arm in arm, those two hissed all the way to the house.

Pa threw up his hands in total frustration. The girls were learning the wiles of the female ways, and Tut and I were on the receiving ends.

One end, spiders. Other end, poison ivy.

Joker Went Berserk

Pa had two working mules. A mule is an offspring between a horse and an ass and can be most temperamental when forced into a job. The only thing worse than a stubborn mule is having one go berserk.

Pa got the mules from old Ben in town. Since we didn't have a lot of money, Pa would drive his wagon, hitched by two horses, into the nearest town, which happened to be fifteen miles from the Crossin, as a crow flies. Pa only ventured into town if he needed something for the farm or found a special item for Ma. Pa was a natural born welder, and his expertise in handling metal was known by those people owning smelters and weld shops. Word of mouth spread rapidly about Pa's talent for the hot metal, which in turn rewarded him nicely with money. Pa made money each time he went into town. In fact, I learned much later in life that Pa was a man of many talents. His knack of picking up a trade, putting his knowledge into a workable situation, and following through on all jobs put him in great demand.

Anyway, Pa came home one day with two mules tied to the back of the wagon. A smile was plastered across his face when Ma greeted him at the door. "I got us some werkin' mules. Thay'll be a big help with th' plowin'. Git aboard, Ma! Let's go git these mules in th' barn. Don't want Joker ta tarn round un head fer town agin'. I been chasin' ol Joker. He dun got loose once un I'm right near tuckered out frum liftin' his rear off'en th' ground. Crazy danged mule ain't all thar. He ran me in th' briar thicket. I was a chasin' him down th' road, jist about ta grab th' tether when he tarned on me un commenced ta chase me, teeth bared. Old Ben told me not ta tarn my back on'em cause he'us a mite shittish lately. He didn't know whut wus ailin' him but somethin' shore nuff wus tickin' him off."

Ma just laughed. "I reckon you'll git him used ta werkin with ye."

"Jist don't let J.D. anywhar near this mule till he's broke in. Between th' two of'em thar jist ain't no tellin' what might happen!"

"Don't fret, Pa. J. D.'s a spendin' th' night with Tut. Grampaw will keep'em busy tonite," Ma told Pa. "Th' girls went ta visit Grammaw and tend Baby Jo fer awhile. Thay outta be back any minute."

Old Nick was the easiest mule to maneuver. It was as though Nick didn't have a care in the world and knew which side of the haystack was his. I guess he figured Pa wasn't such a bad person, or maybe it was because he knew Pa wasn't in a good frame of mind having been chased through briar thickets.

Joker was another story. Getting that mule to move an inch was like moving a mountain. Pa was jerkin' the tether while Ma grappled with his neck. Ma kept sayin', "Pa, this mule has a powerful stink to'em. Are ye sure ye want him in th' barn? He smells like he's been'a wallerin' in hog slop. Cain't we jist tether'em ta th' railin' fer th' night? Come mornin', we can figger out how ta git him outta this cantankerous mood."

"Mite as well, Ma. Don't figger we can git him calmed down tonite."

Pa and Ma smelled worse than a sty. When they got back to the house, Effie Mae and Aunt Sukie had come back from Grammaw's house, took one smell of Pa and Ma and wouldn't let them indoors. Aunt Sukie told Ma she would get the number two tub and fill it with hot water. Aunt Sukie took the tub and placed it on the back stoop while Effie Mae went to the well house and drew five buckets of water. Since the wood cook stove was always hot with coals, it didn't take long for the bath water to heat. Ma and Pa didn't tell the girls about the mules. They wanted to let it be a surprise come morning!

Ma took her turn scrubbing with lye soap, enjoying being pampered by the girls. It had been a long while since Ma was afforded a luxury of taking a bath so early in the evening. Her turn at a bath was usually last one in. Normally the girls would be first, Pa next and then me. I was always next to last cause I made the biggest mess. Actually, I didn't make a mess. Just say we had very clean floors. Ma always seemed to be trailing up the rear. She'd say, "Don't airy mind a bit. Whilst all of ye are a sweatin', I'll be a coolin' off afore I hit th' hay!" I always wondered why Ma made us use the hot water while she enjoyed the cool fresh-drawn well water. The only time Ma bathed in hot water was in the dead of winter. Ma was one smart cookie!

Pa took his bath while Ma prepared supper. Since I was spending the night with Tut and didn't know about the mules, Ma and Pa had a restful night. Well, maybe not so restful. Joker was about to raise old billy nell.

Halfway in the mid-morning hours, Joker began baying. A harnk, harrnk, he harnk, he harnk, eeish he harnk, eeish he harnk. Ma sat bolt right up in bed as the girls came running, lickety split, into their bedroom screaming, "Sumthin's tryin" ta git us! Wake up, Pa! Git th' gun. It's real ugly, Pa. Git th' gun! It's gotta be th' devil. Its ears are real pointed un it's nashing its teeth. Do something Pa, afore it comes back!"

Pa went outside but couldn't find a thing. He walked around the smokehouse, well house, chicken coop, and barn. Everything seemed to be as it should be. Nothing out of order. Even old Joker was still sitting by the rail. Getting back to the house, Pa told Ma the girls must have had a nightmare. There was nothing outside.

"Did ye check all th' out houses, Pa?" the girls said in unison.

"Git back ta bed," Pa yelled, "turn th' pillows over, lay yore heads down and git some shut eye! It'll be mornin' afore I ever git ta sleep." Looking through bleary eyes, he mumbled to Ma, "I've got stickers in my backside un I ain't in nary mood ta traipse out lookin' fer th' devil. Joker is th' only devil I had th' displeasure of meetin' yisterday and I ain't spendin' my sleepin' time ta search fer th' other!"

As usual, Ma and Pa were up before daybreak laying out the day's work. Pa told Ma he needed to go to Grampaw's house to help mend the front stoop. Some of the boards were buckling and needed to be replaced before either one of them got hurt. With Grampaw, Tut and me helping Pa, he wouldn't be gone more than a couple of hours. When he returned home he'd work with Joker. The mule had plenty of water and hay and would be okay for a couple of hours. He told Ma to yell real loud if she needed any help. When a body yelled in the holler, it was loud, real loud! A yell didn't have anywhere to go except bounce off the hills. It was bound to attract someone's attention.

Ma said not to worry. She and the girls needed to scrub clothes and do some housework. Ma woke the girls and told them to eat their breakfast, straighten the bed and dust the floor while she drew water from the well. Ma prepared the scrub tub and piled sorted, dirty clothes on the stoop. Whites in one, colors in the other. While the water was heating, she took the lye soap, dipped it in vinegar and rubbed stains with the solution. Ma then sat down and sipped coffee. By the time she drank her coffee the water was hot enough to wash clothes. The girls and Ma worked the better part of the morning getting the wash out on the clothesline. Clothes always smelled so fresh and looked so pretty flowing in the early morning breeze. Ma always took great pride in taking care of the family. Everything she did was done with great love. We could tell she was a happy person because she sang with every step she took.

Ma sat down on the front porch but didn't stay there for

long. Ka thump! Eesh shaw, eesh shaw: Joker had bolted right beside Ma. His teeth were showing through the wide, smiling lips, ears twitching with every eesh shaw. Ma's eyes got the size of saucers, her mouth gaped open and she leaped behind a table. Joker was inching his way toward Ma, throwing his head side to side.

At the same time, Effie Mae and Aunt Sukie walked upon the ever-present Joker, let out a blood-curdling scream and shot off the front porch like firecrackers. They plowed into one another before going in opposite directions. Effie Mae went north, Aunt Sukie went south, and Joker went for Ma. Ma leaped off the porch, screaming at the top of her lungs with every step she took while the girls were yelling, "Run, Ma, run!" Joker was hot on Ma's trail and a little too close for comfort. Joker was kicking up a small powerful dust bowl with every lunge toward Ma's backside. Ma just kept on running, dodging Joker's determined advancing blows. Just in the nick of time Ma reached the outhouse. Joker plopped down right in front of the two-holer, holding the door shut with his body and rubbing his neck on the door.

Joker must have known what he was doing. He stood up, lowered his head and ran straight for the clothesline. His head was jerking side to side, both back feet kicking hard enough to knock a body into next year, and then he lunged for the clean clothes. Joker had gone berserk! Joker was giving the clean clothes a right good flailing! Running under the clothesline, his head got hung inside Pa's underwear. One underwear leg was wrapped around his neck, the other one shoved down over his head. Joker couldn't see a blasted thing. Laundry was scattered all over the yard, tables were upended, Ma's coffee cup was hurled to the ground, the girls were up a tree and Ma had locked herself in the outhouse. Everyone was raising Cain!

Even though the ruckus didn't last long, it seemed like Joker was on the warpath for hours. He upended everything in sight, even though he couldn't see where he was going. Ma was screaming for the girls, the girls were screaming for Ma. Joker was sitting down, baying a muffled eesh shaw.

Pa, Tut, Grampaw and I came running home. We could hear all the screaming. In fact, a few of the hill folk had met us in the field wondering what in tarnation was happening. Pa was in a fine fit when he saw the havoc Joker had created. I was none too happy 'cause I missed the ruckus. Grampaw sauntered up to the porch and sat down. Tut hid behind Grampaw!

The girls screamed at Pa, "We told you, Pa! Thet wus th' devil we seen last nite! Whut is thet stupid lookin' thang? We ain't gittin' outta this tree, Pa! Ma's locked herself in th' outhouse un won't come out. Thet thang's got green teeth, Pa!"

"Whar's th' other one?" Pa asked the girls.

"You mean thar's two'a them devils?" the girls screamed. They started screaming and screaming and wouldn't shut up.

Ma peeked out the outhouse door. Boy was she mad! Her eyes shot fire, and if she had a gun, she would have killed that mule. "Jist lookit my fresh wash! Why, I ain't ever gonna git them clean! Me un th' girls werked hard all mornin' long. Jist lookit my wash!" she kept saying.

Grampaw grabbed Tut by the nape of his neck and said, "We're goin' home. No need in stayin' here! Fer a man in his proper mind, well, this jist ain't no place ta be rite now!"

I walked up to Joker, took the underwear off Jokers' head and led him to the barn.

"J. D., how in thunder did ye git him ta calm down?" Pa questioned.

"Shucks, Pa, twern't nothin'! I jist took a big piece'a splinter outta his neck. He wus hurtin' Pa. He musta been whackin' his neck on a barn board ta git a sticker thet big in his neck. No wonder he went nuts. He didn't ritely mean no harm. He wus jist trin' ta tell ye thet he needed tendin'. Please, Pa, don't take'em back to Ben. Let's keep'em. He'll be a fine work mule.

Please, Pa."

Pa just looked at me and shook his head. He didn't know if it was one devil speaking to another or simple human kindness that brought old Joker to his senses. Whatever it was, Joker and I became best friends. I would smile at Joker, and Joker would smile back. God surely works in mysterious ways.

Going to Church

We didn't have a proper church house. In fact, we were lucky if a preacher got to our neck of the hills once a month. The preacher man was on a circuit. A circuit means the poor old preacher had to fill all the needs of everyone in or near the holler for miles around. Trouble is, he'd have to ride horseback twenty some odd miles over hilly terrain come rain or shine and divide up his time between different stops. One Sunday he'd be here and the rest of the Sundays he'd be someplace else.

Word would spread like wildfire through the hills when someone got wind of the preacher coming to the Crossin'. It was a very special day. Everybody in the hills would dress in their finest "Sunday come to meetin'" clothes, pack a good-sized meal in a basket for the "picnic on the grounds" and not worry about doing chores. Pa loved to say, "No werkin' on th Sabbath."

We'd all meet at Mr. Matlock's general store for the preaching. People would drive their wagons to the store, hitch the team to a near by tree and wait for the preacher. It didn't matter if we had to wait an hour or so, nobody cared! Everyone had a good time just gossipin'. Besides, everybody knew if the preacher did show up, it might be four or five hours before he shut up!

When we got wind that the preacher was coming down the bend, Ma would grab us kids and make us sit straight-faced to greet the preacher. Even though Ma would spread out blankets for us to sit on, it was rough on the backside. Sitting still very long on the old, hard wagon till the preacher stopped saying his "hell fire and damned nation" sermon made all the kids squirm and snicker. Me and Tut would poke each other in the ribs, just for the fun of it! Ma would say, "Mind yeself, now, ye mite jist larn sumthin'. Iffen ye don't stop thet rite now, ye'll find yerself behind th' woodshed!"

When the preacher arrived we realized he was not the same man we had in the past. Nobody knew him but welcomed him anyway. As he began preaching in a high-pitched tone, he would fling his arms in the air with a Bible in one hand and a fist made of the other. When he got all fired up in the full swing preachin' mode, and he kept hearin' all the amens being shouted, it just put fuel in his mouth. I thought, "We musta been the worst sinners alive."

He was a preachin' about the devil and how the devil had a foothold in the corner of our lives. "Cain't let th' devilish ways drift amongst th' tip o'th' tongue. He'll jerk ye down through th' gates of th' fiery hell and burn ye soul frum yer very bein'. Don't touch th' likker', smash yer devilish ways now afore yer condemned ta a life o'sin!"

Lots of the people would commence squirmin' 'cause the preacher was layin' it on just a mite heavy against drinkin' the hooch and cussin'. All the big folks in the hollers would snitch a swaller' or two, even Pa and Ma if they were ailin', and cussin' seemed to be a natural thing to do! Not taking the Lord's name in vain. That was never done! The preacher went from preachin' to meddlin'. He preached on and on and on. Two or three hours went by and he was still talking!

There was something about this man, something I did not like! I couldn't exactly put my finger on what it was. He had squatty eyes, a big old round face and a fake laugh. You know the kind of laugh? It's when you try to laugh at something and you know it's not funny but you force out a "pretend" laugh and hope nobody notices. I poked Tut in the ribs and said, "Tut, I shore nuff don't like thet man."

Grammaw overheard what I said, jerked me out of the

wagon, pulled me behind the general store and wailed the tar out of me. I was feeling some of that "hellfire" the preacher was spouting. We walked back to the wagon and Grammaw said, "Mind yer manners J.D., or we'll find us a bigger stick."

Climbing back on the wagon, I heard the preacher say, "That's whut I wus a talkin' about. Spare th' rod un spoil th' child. Ye gotta fix'em un putt'em in thar place. Seen but not heard."

We sang a few songs and passed the hat for the preacher, and he commenced to pray the prayer. All those thees and thous had me messed up. All I understood was, "Dear Lord" and "amen"!

By that time everyone was hungry. My stomach was playing a tune on my backbone but I needed, right then and there, to find a place to relieve myself of backed-up water—the kind of backed-up water that if you took a deep breath, everything would shoot out your nose. I walked behind a big tree and proceeded to do "the pause that refreshed." When I had completed my "pause," I began walking back to the picnic area.

Looking over my shoulder, I saw the preacher open up his dirty old black coat, take out a goose-necked bottle and guzzle down two or three big gulps. He wiped his mouth with his sleeve and burped. He was standing there, legs spread slightly apart, weaving back and forth. I knew he was up to no good, but I didn't say a word to anyone.

Before the picnic was over, I told Ma it would be nice to ask him if he would like to visit us the next time he came to the Crossin' to preach. Since I wasn't very nice today and still feeling the "crossed side of Grammaw," it would be my way of saying I was sorry. Ma said she thought it was a good idea and invited the preacher. In fact, she told all the hill folk to meet at our house for the next Sunday sermon. His response was with a nasty, smirky little smile: "I can hardly wait, Mam."

Never in my wildest thought did I realize just what was in store for him!

Let's Git Outta Here

Me and Tut did some pretty danged stupid things. One time, I recall, nearly got us killed.

I'm not sure but I think there were about twenty-some-odd families that lived in or around the hollers. Some lived close to the Crossin'. Other folks lived pretty far away. We knew everybody in those parts and never had to lock our doors at night. Just didn't make any sense to lock doors. Besides, nobody had any locks! The only way to lock a door was by putting a board across the inside of the door, sort of like a chair being jimmied up against a doorknob.

Lots of people were coming to the holler. More people than the hollers had room for. I guess they were hunting a place to squat. More likely, looking for a piece of land to grow food to keep from starving to death. I'm here to tell you, everybody was in the same fix! Pa always said, "People are a fearin'. Iffen we could git people ta stop shovin' un a hatin', th' world would shore nuff be a better place ta live." We weren't feared of living; it was the fear of dying that shook up everybody. The fear of the unknown, that's what it was!

Anyway, getting back to the story. Well, me and Tut were just plain bored! We decided to strike out and find something to do. We didn't know exactly what, but between the two of us, we wouldn't be bored for long. We poked around the Crossin' and si-fogged down the dirt road in the direction of the "big city." We heard stories about the "city folk" and about them being so "uppity" with their shiny "autiemobiles." Shoot, we knew all about those things. In fact, we sat in one of them. We weren't invited to sit in it, we just did it! Got blessed out for it too. Another thing we knew about was the bank robbers headin' off to the woods to get away from the law.

We figured we'd better let someone know where we were going, so we turned around and headed home. Pa and Grampaw were working in the field and were busy talking about something that happened yesterday. We hollered that we were going to walk a spell down the road toards the "city." We were always joking about heading off for the city and Pa knew it. Pa chuckled out to us, " Better watch out fer th' crooks. Thay jist mite shoot ye!"

We didn't pay any mind to what Pa said, mainly because we couldn't hear him. We really didn't care what he said; we were just too busy gabbing and being excited about our venture. Me and Tut were having the best time. The old dirt road was mighty dusty and not very smooth. It veered around big rocks jutting out of the ground and was full of potholes. Some of the potholes were large because of the rainy season. The rain would swoop down the mountainside, force boulders to fall and gouge out holes bigger than the road itself.

We found an old can and started to kick it down the road. We played kick the can till our toes began to cramp. We wore what Ma called "hand me downs" from other kids in the holler which were a size too small for our feet, and we were wearing bigger holes in holes that were already there. Besides, we had kicked the old rusty can to smithereens and it balled up in a heap of old metal. We'd find something else to do!

It was hot outside. Really hot! Every now and then, a breeze would blow through the tops of the trees and the sunlight would flicker through the branches. Shadows of tree limbs would dance around us, making everything look prettier than it was. Even the little wild daisy flowers would poke their heads up trying to get sunshine. It really was a beautiful sight, even through all the accumulated dust. We hadn't had a good soaking rain in a spell, and we needed one really bad.

Tut started to flap his jaws and made me forget what I was looking at. Tut was hungry! As a matter of fact, my belly was growling too. We decided it was too far to the city without food in our bellies so we turned around and headed for home.

All of a sudden, we could hear shotgun blasts. Everybody knew what noise from a shotgun blast meant. Hit the dirt! We figured someone was hunting when they shouldn't be hunting or getting the pattern of the shotgun pellets. Maybe they were just practicing. We just hoped whoever was doing the shooting wouldn't spray us with the pellets. Those pellets would sting like a hornet, not to mention kill ya!

The popping sounded a couple of times, then stopped. We could hear a roaring sound, like rocks striking a tin roof on an out building, and the sound just kept getting louder. Lots of dust started flying through the air. It was coming through the woods 'cause the breeze was blowing it our way.

"Let's see whut's goin' on," Tut whispered. Tut crossed the ditch with me hot on his heels. The leaves were awfully dry from the lack of rain and crunched under our feet. Climbing up the steep hill, we grabbed low-lying tree limbs to secure our footing. We tried to walk as softly as we could and pull ourselves up the hill without being heard and avoid stepping on rattlesnakes that loved the underbrush.

Reaching the top of the hill, we could see the side of an old shack. The shack looked as though it could fall down any minute. Some of the clapboards were hanging sideways, and the roof was full of holes. The front porch had a couple of planks to walk on, and part of the front door had rotted away. We crept up near a window and tried to look inside. There was too much dirt on the window to peek inside, and we were afraid to wipe it off, thinking somebody might see or hear us. We tiptoed toward the back of the shack and heard someone start yelling real loud, "I told you, you do it my way! I'm the boss, get that straight, I'm the boss!" Whoever was doing the talking was walking on loose planks toward us. We quickly crawled under the back stoop. At that point, we knew we had poked our noses where they didn't belong. We just hoped we'd have noses if we got out of this alive!

Tut poked me in the ribs and pointed to the north corner of the house. We could see tires on one of those new fandangled automobiles. The tires looked awfully big from the angle we were laying. The automobile was black with a low, wide running board. It had two doors. The driver's side door was wide open and the trunk was raised. We knew that anyone driving one of those things wouldn't be living in this shack!

There were two brown horses in a makeshift pen by the north side of the automobile. The horses were running back and forth, whinnying and snorting. They were very uneasy.

The screaming and yelling started getting louder. Next thing we knew, someone fired a shotgun. The pellets went clean through the back door. The force of the pellets sprayed the trees in front of us. Then came the second blast. Tut and I were scared to death, and Tut peed all over himself. We were wishing we were anywhere, anywhere but here!

There had to be at least three people in the shack. One woman and two men. They were fighting and cussing a blue streak. Pretty soon, one of the men ran out the door toward the "auttiemobile." The woman kept yelling, "No, no, no." The next sound was a shotgun blast and the sound of pellets hitting the automobile. Then, a thud against the dirt. The woman commenced to scream. The other man was pulling her toward the automobile while she was putting up a fight as he shoved her to the ground. He grabbed her by her hair and forced her into the automobile. The roar of the engine commenced and dirt and rocks were flung all over the place by the spinning tires.

The silence was awful! Me and Tut scrambled out from under the stoop after we were sure they were gone. We crept up to the man lying on the ground. He wasn't very old and was dressed in a black suit with a big wide lapel. His shoes were fanciful, shiny speckled things. The hat he was wearing was knocked off when his head hit the ground. We turned him over and found out that he was stone cold dead!

Me and Tut could hear that automobile coming back up the old dirt road. We ran as fast as our legs could carry us and jumped on the two horses in the pen. The horses were spooked from all the shooting and were as ready as we were to get out of there right now! Our hands were shaking so bad we could barely hold on to their manes. Both horses were big, and we had a hard time holding them still while we desperately climbed on their backs. We both were as white as a sheet. I could feel the blood surge through my veins, and my head was full of roaring sounds. Everything had a muffled tone. I could see Tut screaming at me but I couldn't hear him. Tut kicked me in the leg and it brought me to my senses. We dug our feet into the sides of the horses and hung onto their manes for dear life!

It's a good thing the horses knew where they were going, 'cause we were so scared, our sense of direction was turned around. The horses headed down the side of the mountain. We went through briar patches, slid on loose soil and we got all scratched up from tree limbs smacking us. We were a right mess! I looked at Tut, he looked at me and we both laughed hysterically. The two of us had spider webs wrapped in our hair, and the dirt around our mouths looked as though we had been eating mud pies. Sweat, fear and dust do not mix!

We reached the bottom of the hill. There's the road! But we were completely turned around. The horses didn't come down the hill the same way we went up. Tut didn't know where we were, and I didn't see any of the little wild yellow daisy flowers in sight. My mind was plastered with, "Think, J. D., think!" Then I remembered Pa always telling me, "It's easy ta git tarned round back'ards in these hills, but iffen ye go one direction un nary see anythang whut looks familiar, tarn round un go in th' tuther direction."

We turned the horses around and rode'm hard. In a few minutes, there was the Crossin'. We passed the Crossin' with dust flying. We reached the clearing where Pa and Grandpa were working and began yelling at the top of our lungs. Pa and Grandpa saw us coming and knew something was mighty wrong. "Whut'sa matter? Whar'd ya'll git them horses?" Grampaw yelled as he jerked us off the horses.

We commenced to tell them about what we'd seen and how we were afraid that someone might have seen us riding off the hill with the horses. Pa told us to stay with Grampaw, and he ran to the house. As he grabbed his shotgun from the fireplace holder, he told Ma, Grammaw and the girls to stay in the house and jimmy up the doors. "Don't ye come outta this house till I git back! Ma, git yer hand gun un keep it close by. Don't ye dare open this door till ye know fer shore it's me."

Grampaw, Pa, Tut and I rode to the general store and told Mr. Matlock to ring up the sheriff in the city. He needed to get up to the Crossin' as soon as possible. It would be awhile before the sheriff got to the Crossin', so we commenced to tell our story again—this time a little slower.

It seems like we waited forever on the sheriff, but pretty soon he drove up. He asked us a lot of questions, and we piled in his automobile and drove to the place where we climbed the hill. Since we didn't pass any lanes on the way, the sheriff said we'd drive on a little further 'cause he'd noticed a lane about two miles on up the road. When we got to the lane, the sheriff turned the big old automobile hard to the left. We commenced up what appeared to be a pig trail. It was real bumpy and we had to veer over into the brushy banks to avoid hitting big rocks. When we got to the top of the hill it was quiet! Very quiet!

Nobody was there. We all climbed out of the automobile. The sheriff had his pistol drawn, and Pa had his shotgun. They knew we were telling the truth because there were tire tracks and a sign of a scuffle. The old door was hanging on a creaky hinge. Bits and splintery pieces of the door were lying on the ground. Inside the shack, they found uneaten food scattered about and tables overturned. Cigarette butts were ground into the wood floor. Going back outside, the sheriff found a pool of blood where the body had been sprawled across the ground.

Since it was getting dark, the sheriff drove us back to the general store. He told us to go on home and tend to the two horses till he could sort this mess out. He'd get some deputies and come back tomorrow at first light. Well, me and Tut was ready to go home. We stayed close to Pa and Grampaw the rest of the day.

We never did find out what happened to those people and hoped they'd never come to the holler again. The sheriff did tell us that the man who was shot might not have been dead but… if he was dead, the folk who came back for him didn't want anyone to find out who he was. "Just keep an eye open. Whoever it was might come back. May never know exactly what happened. Goodnight folks, thanks for the help." The sheriff drove away.

Well, me and Tut shore nuff knew one danged thang! We weren't ready for the likes of the city jist yet, or for what came next!

Lil' Beedy Eyes In The Mason Jars

Daddy said, "Have I told you about the muskedines yet?"

"I don't think so," I laughed. "What about the muskedines?"

Well, it was sometime in August and hotter than hell! The muskedine vines were loaded with the mouthwater'nist wild grapes that we had tasted in a long while. They were sweet and real plump from the over abundance of spring rain. The rain must have soaked down really close to the roots for them to be so sweet in the hot weather. Hardly any of the wild grapes were dried on the vines. We had tons of them.

Since Effie Mae and Aunt Sukie wanted to help Ma and Grammaw with the juicin' of the grapes to make jelly and grape butter, and they knew which of the grapes to pick, Tut and I traipsed along with'em to select the best ones. I bet we picked a bushel of those muskedines! Ma would boast as to how proud she was of us kids, braving the chiggers and ticks to pick the muskedines. "Biskits'll shore nuff taste good this winter with th' jelly'n butter slathered on'em."

Me and Tut asked Ma if we could help with the canning. Aunt Sukie made fun of us, sayin', "Dumb ol' boys cain't can. It's fer us wimmin. Ain't thet rite, Ma?"

Ma said, "Not rite now, J. D. Iffen we need any help, we'll shore holler fer ye, though."

Me and Tut watched them sort the canning jars, wash them and rinse them in hot boiling water and leave them set full of hot water till they were ready to use them. Then they'd sort and wash the wild grapes, put them in a big blackened copper kettle, add a certain amount of water, and squash the muskedines till they were real mushy. Cook'em, cool'em, strain'em and then cook'em again. The heat from the old cook stove was so hot it would choke a horse or make a preacher cuss! That sure was a lot of hard work for just a few masons of jelly. It seemed as though there was an easier way to make jelly, maybe a short cut. If Tut and I could figure out a short cut, we could show up those bossy, know-it-all girls.

Ma piled at least twelve mason jars in a basket. She told Tut and me to take away the jars with the cracked rims and dump them in the cistern. Ma said how hard she worked, sewing stuff to trade for the jars at Mr. Matlock's general store. It was a shame to have to throw them away. The jars looked okay to me and Tut. They had a few chips in the rims, but other than that, they looked fit to use. The lids were a funny-looking contraption: A rubber ring and a glass lid with a wire latch. The wire latch folded over the lid and connected under the jar rim.

Me and Tut snatched the jars, an old washtub, a bucket full of muskedines and a wire screen. We didn't want Ma to know what we were doing, so we took everything down to the creek. Since we didn't know if someone would be at the swimming hole, we decided to do our canning at the wading area. After Tut scrubbed everything real good and dumped all the muskedines on the screen to drain, I took my hands and fists and smashed'em till they were pulp. We poured in some sugar and something Ma had put on the table. We didn't know what the "something" was but figured it was for making jelly. That "something" was in a clump and had a weird smell to it. We crumbled it up real good and stirred everything together. Our mouths were watering something fierce! We just knew we would be successful in our first canning attempt. The peelings were the best part of the grape, and we crammed them in the jars with the juice. We packed those Mason jars with the prettiest purple mash we'd ever seen. We made sure the seals were on real tight. The only thing we didn't do? Cook them!

We put all the filled jars in the wash tub and sneaked back

to the house. It had to be our secret. We peeked around the corner of the house to see where everyone was. Cat sakes, they were still cooking that mess. That old kettle had turned blacker and was still boilin'. I wanted to tell them they were workin' too hard, but I held my tongue.

Ma always said to keep the jars out of a draft and put them where they would stay cool. Well, the best place to put our jars would be way back under the front porch. They wouldn't be in a draft or in direct sunshine. The crawl space would be perfect, and I told Tut to keep an eye out for anyone coming near the front porch while I ran in the house and grabbed up one of Pa's old work shirts. Didn't figure he'd miss it. I sneaked back outside and we crawled under the porch. Tut scooted the basket while I pulled it as far under the porch as we thought necessary. Couldn't go very far under there, though. There was a slope where the porch met the front door. Knowing the jars wouldn't sit upright, we put them halfway between the step up and front door. We laid our Masons on Pa's old shirt. There was a little flicker of sunshine coming through the porch cracks, but we figured a little sunshine wouldn't do any harm.

For the next two or three weeks, me and Tut would examine the jars. We could see the grapes "werkin" and sometimes a mite too hard! Every now and then, foam would come to the top of the jars and the grapes would dance around in the juice. Funny thing, Ma's grapes never did that. We saw some of the juice trickle from the cracks in the rims but figured that was because we were shaking the jars too much. We decided to leave them alone for a spell. Besides, Ma was wondering how in the world we were getting the fronts of our britches and shirts so dirty. Well, we knew it was from crawling in and out from under the porch.

Tut kept telling me how the Masons were looking a mite spooky. Tut would say, "J. D., I reckon not ta be a crawlin' under thet porch no more. Them jars keep'a lookin' at me wiff beedy lil' grape eyes!"

That Saturday night we found out the preacher would be in the holler for preaching on Sunday. We stayed up for a spell, poppin' corn and drinkin' apple cider. Pa and Grampaw were playing the fiddle and Ma and Grammaw were dancing around acting silly. The girls were trying to learn how to dance, Baby Jo was crawlin' around, and me and Tut were roughhousing. Since it was getting real late, Grammaw, Grampaw, Tut and Baby Jo would spend the night. Ma and Grammaw decided to get up at first light and cook a chicken or two, along with poke greens and biscuits for the picnic after the preaching.

While they were cooking, Pa and Grampaw would scythe down tall grass in preparation for the pretty quilts being laid on the ground for sitting, eating upon, visiting with friends, or maybe even taking a nap. They would put an old table on the porch for all the food. When hill folk cooked, they brought what they had. It might be beans, dandelion greens, biscuits, or jowl. No one had a lot, but what they had really tasted good. Yup! Come first light, they would get this done.

For now, since it was getting real late, Ma made me and Tut clear out the stuff she stored in the loft. "Fetch thet stuff and pile it in th' corner thar. Bring them quilts rite here and foldem' over fer a pallet. Me and Pa'll nest down here, whilst Grammaw un Grampaw sleep in th' bed. Ya boys'll have ta take ta th' loft. Baby Jo can sleep wiff Effie Mae and Aunt Sukie. Don't ye boys be'a horsin' round up thar. Yer liable ta fall rite through th' railin'. Mornin's gonna be here afore we know it. Git yer nite shirts on un git ta bed." Having said all that, she blew out the coal oil lantern.

In the dark it isn't easy to poke on an old nightshirt. I just hated those nightshirts! During the night if you turned over in a hurry, those blamed old things would crawl up your back, get twisted around your neck and nearly choke you to death. Your arms felt as though they were in a vise cutting off any kind of circulation, while your rear-end stuck out for all the world to see. We wore skivvies, but somehow those nightshirts had a way of getting tangled up with the skivvies. If it wasn't choking you to death, it was hung up in the skivvies, mashing the other end of the body. Besides, it wasn't proper for Tut and me, not to mention Grampaw and Pa, to be wearing those silly-looking things. We looked right sissyfied.

Anyway, we went to sleep. I don't know how long we had been asleep when we heard noises. Tut and I crawled down the ladder. I saw Pa go into the bedroom and wake Grampaw. Grampaw reached under the bed for a long stick and stuck it at the top of the window to keep anyone outside from raising the window. Pa grabbed the shotgun from the mantle and crawled to the front door. We thought they had flipped a noodle. I was about to ask what was going on when Grampaw whispered, "Keep yore mouths shut! Stay out of th' moonlight. Git ta th' floor!" By that time, Ma, Grammaw and the girls had all clumped together in a dark corner.

Grampaw got down on his all fours and sneaked over to where Pa was crouched. Naturally, Tut and I followed suit. Pa had pushed a table up against the front door and was peeking out the window. "Whut's goin' on?" I whispered.

Grampaw said, "I told ya ta shut yore mouth. Iffen ye don't, thay're liable ta shut it fer ye!"

It got real quiet. All we could hear was each other breathing. All of a sudden, a shotgun blast hit the front door. It laid a fear clean up in my throat! "It's gotta be them crooks, Pa, thay've come back a huntin' me un Tut!"

Pa yelled out the window and told them to get away before he started shooting. Whoever was out there didn't say a word. Pa fired a blast out the window toward the front yard. A few minutes later, it got real quiet again. Best we could see was from the light of the moon. It didn't appear that anyone was too close to the porch, and we guessed that Pa had scared them away when he fired his shotgun. Grampaw said they must have been on the front porch cause he could smell the "likker." Maybe they decided not to mess with Pa. About an hour went by and we decided to get back to sleep. We slept with one eye open the rest of the night. Grampaw didn't know if he should sleep in the bed or under it.

Sunday morning crept up all too fast. The aroma of coffee, eggs and jowl woke us up. Frankly, we were glad the sun came up and were ready to get out of the bed, even if it was a Sunday. We all sat down to breakfast. It was so nice to have everyone together. I loved having Tut, Grammaw, Grampaw and Baby Jo in the same house and often wished they'd come down off the mountain and live with us. It would take a powerful lot of talking or an act of God to move Grammaw from that mountain.

While Ma and Grammaw were cooking the chickens and getting ready for the Sunday picnic, Pa and Grampaw were out in the front yard looking for spent shotgun shells. Tut and I went out to help them but we didn't find any shells. We found some glass on the front porch and saw where the likker had spilled. Somebody was there all right; they had been a drinkin' and you could smell it 'cause it soaked the porch planks and left a powerful stink. Since we didn't find any sign of anyone still hanging around, and no one was lurking in the barn or out houses, Pa and Grampaw went about setting up the picnic stuff.

Ma yelled for us to get cleaned up for the preaching. We poured some water in a pan and started scrubbing. "Don't ferget them ears. Make shore ye git th' backs of'em too. Don't want anybody sayin' ye ain't clean. Dust offen them shoes. Make shore yore britches cuffs ain't got no dust in'em too!" It was funny to hear Ma yell those words since I remembered a phrase from the preacher. It was about how all of us were made out of dust and how we would return to dust when we went to our rewards. Well, if we were made out of dust, who in sam hill would see a little bit of dirt? Old eagle eye Ma...that's who!

Well, the yard began to fill with wagons, men, women and children. Pretty soon that old preacher, the one I didn't like, showed up and the preaching began. As expected, he'd flail his arms and shake his voice. This went on for nearly an hour. I guess he must have been hungry 'cause his preaching stopped shorter than usual. Everyone gathered around the vittles, Pa blessed the food and we began having a real good time. All of us kids would play hide and seek, king of the mountain or kick the can. The menfolk talked about the weather, how the small gardens were growing and when the weather would change. The women would show off their quilts, discuss the changes of life or how the kids were doing. The preacher was sitting on the front porch talking with Grampaw.

Several hours went by and all the folks went home. Everyone except the preacher! Tut overheard him tell Grampaw how he needed to stay behind and visit with a neighbor lady. Something about how her husband was ailing and he needed to check on them. Tut knew right away the preacher was full of the devil. Tut was about to tell me everything he'd overheard when Grampaw said, "Don't be a flappin' them jaws, boy. Ye best keep yore mouth shut. Don't go a tellin' everthang ye know'er hear. Iffen the good Lord's a willin', He'll be th' one ta set thangs straight. Ya boys, git on now. Go find sumthin' ta do."

Tut and I went down to the barn. We climbed up in a pile of hay and hoped to get some sleep and let our bloated stomachs ease up a bit. We had eaten too much and were tired from not getting enough sleep the night before.

About that time, all hell broke loose. Ma was screaming and Grammaw was spittin' and sputterin'. Pa flung that barn door open, snatched me off the hay, jerked Tut up by the ears and drug us through old wet cow patties and thistle bushes in the pasture. We didn't even know what we'd done and didn't have time to ask. Pa didn't say a word but we knew right away that something was mighty wrong! Then the sound of gunshot blasts filled our ears. We kept telling Pa to hit the dirt, the crooks came back. Pa kept on dragging us. Then a downdraft hit us. Phew! It smelled like a hundred wine stills a brewing at the same time.

When we reached the front porch, Grampaw was laughing so hard that tears were streaming down his face. Grammaw and Ma were cleaning up the preacher's britches and shirt. The preacher was wrapped up in one of those old nightshirts and you could see his skivvies hanging down around his knees. His legs were a mottled purplish color and he was shaking to beat the band. The porch was a mess! It was speckled purple and slivers of glass were stuck to the bottom of the porch planks. The rafters above his head was dripping blotches of muskedine peelings on top of his head.

Cat sakes! Me and Tut's canning had exploded all over the preacher. Pa was crawling really, really slow up close to the porch with a long cane pole, whacking the Mason jars trying to finish off the exploding. Pa was ducking every time one of the Mason jars began to hiss.

Unbeknownst to me and Tut, we had whipped up some of the best tasting muskedine wine that Grampaw had ever tasted. While Pa was whacking those jars, Grampaw had sneaked a jar that hadn't popped the lid. He was sipping and giggling at the same time. Pa yelled for us to "Git in th' house. We got sum talkin' ta do." While Pa was giving us the what fors and saying how the preacher didn't take kindly to that kind of nonsense, Grampaw yelled for us look out the window.

Under the oak tree sat the preacher. He was wrapped up in that old nightshirt like a mummy. He was guzzling down some of the muskedine wine. Thinking that no one was looking, he'd peek around the small tree trunk and take another swig. Pretty soon he sauntered up to the house. We listened to him say how wrong it is to be making and drinking the devils brew and if we continued, our souls would head straight to hell. Well, if that were the case, he'd be right along with us.

Ma handed the preacher his britches and shirt. He had to go. "Gotta visit with th' neighbor lady and her man." Pa and Grampaw looked at one another and winked. Tut took his bony old elbow and jabbed me in the ribs and whispered, "Thet's whut I wus trien ta tell ya. She ain't got no old man!"

As the preacher stepped on the porch, the last Mason jar exploded and hit the preacher slap dab on the front of his clean britches. He began to rant and rave. Grampaw looked at Pa and said, "Serves 'em rite! Beins how he's always a tellin' us not ta do….and he does! I guess th' good Lord shore nuff decided ta set him straight." That preacher never came back!

Interlude with Daddy

As usual, the next day I went to see Daddy. With my pencil and paper in hand, ready to write down the next story, I noticed a crowd of elderly men and women. They were inching themselves very slowly toward Daddy's room. Some of them were in wheelchairs and others were steadying themselves with canes or walkers. It was a sight to behold. These little old, frail men and women had heard about Daddy telling stories and wanted to listen.

Daddy's room began filling very quickly. His room wasn't very large. In fact, he shared a room with another gentleman who was claustrophobic. This gentleman needed air and space and was becoming very irate. After calming the gentleman down, I went to the nurses' station and began explaining the situation. One of the nurses' aids said that the hallway shouldn't be too crowded in case of an emergency. She told me to wait a few minutes at the nurses' station. She would be right back. Within a few minutes, the activities director came upon the loudspeaker. She announced, "Anyone wanting to listen to stories, meet in the dining room in ten minutes." I told Daddy about the problem and requested his presence in the dining room. Before too long, the dining room was almost filled. There were those people who, for whatever reason, couldn't make it to the dining room. That problem could be corrected. Daddy would have a microphone and they would pipe the stories directly to those who were unable to get out of bed and wished to hear the stories. I was told, however, some of the elderly people might not respond to the stories and if need be, the PA system would have interruptions with calls for assistance. Telling them I understood, I walked back to the dining room and began talking to Daddy.

"Daddy, I know you did unbelievable things as a child but did you ever do any hard, physical labor?"

"Did I do any hard, physical labor? Believe me, I did my share of hard work. The work back then was back-breaking, hot and almost continuous. Sure, we had our fun times and I naturally sluffed off like any other kid, but if there was work to be done, I worked! Pa knew if I was to become a man, I had to learn everything. That meant learning how to plow, hoe, feed the critters and anything else. Even helping all the hill folk, when need be. I even learned about who was in control!"

This is what happened one day...

God Was In Control

Back when I was growing up, times were hard. When I say hard, I mean there were times when food was scarce and people didn't know where their next meal would come from. We weren't rich by any means. We had a fair piece of land that Grampaw had given Ma and Pa, but the only place to lay seed was in part of the pasture on the east side of the house. The rest of the land was in timber and too hilly to do much planting.

When Ma and Pa came to the holler, they didn't have any critters except for the two horses pulling the wagon. If Grampaw hadn't given Pa an old sow, two piglets and two cows when they got settled in the holler, they might have starved to death.

Anyway, one early spring morning, Pa rattled me out of bed to get started with the day's work. The sun had peeked over the mountain and you could feel the steam rising from the ground. The night hadn't cooled the valley as it usually did. The atmosphere was strange, and I had an ominous, dark feeling about the day as I watched the sky cast a greenish-red tint through gloomy haze circling the hollers.

Ma handed us a jug of water and we headed toward the field. I carried a pitchfork and the jug. Pa had a scythe in one hand and a bushel basket and a hoe in the other. The scythe was a contraption for cutting down weeds or grains. It was half mooned with a real sharp razor blade, about three feet long and as wide a man's hand. The blade was attached to a handle almost as long as a man's leg. In order to use the scythe, you had to get a rhythm going, like an army cadence: "Lay the blade down on the ground, give a swing the grass comes down. Lift it up and lay it down, pretty soon you find the ground." Pa had the rhythm! With every whack, Pa would lay open a bare spot the size of a yard stick.

As Pa cut down the grass, I would shove the pitchfork under the grass and with a big heave, pile it into small heaps. It couldn't be piled too high because the grass needed to "cure." If you didn't cure it just right, the heat and moisture inside the grass blades would ignite and cause a fire. This grass would be dried out and used for hay, come winter. It would be used as fodder for the cows, horses and donkeys.

While Pa kept cutting the grass, I would take the hoe and pound the blade into the soil. My job was to get some of the grass roots out of the ground and put them in the bushel basket. When the basket was full, I would take them to the house, shake off any dirt left on the roots, spread them out to dry, and head back to the field. Ma would use the roots as kindling in the cook stove or fireplace. Those roots would catch fire in a hurry.

Pa would get pretty far ahead of me and stop. "Cain't stop fer too long, now. Git yer breath un wipe yore brow. This here stuff's gotta be done afore we can hitch up th' plowin' mule." We had cleared about one fourth of the new garden spot. Pa wanted to extend our old garden because it wasn't a great big garden, just big enough to feed us and have stuff left over for Ma and the girls to can. We always shared with Grammaw, Grampaw, Tut and Baby Jo. Pa always helped some of the folks in the holler as well. Having a larger garden would make more work for us, but in the long run, helping others always made Pa proud.

By now, the sun was really beating down with blistering heat. We wore old straw hats to deflect the sun's rays, but that didn't keep the heat from penetrating deep under our clothing. Since we didn't have gloves to wear, we'd wrap our hands in old rags or shove them inside a worn-out sock. We'd soak an old rag with water, wring it out, and lay it across the back of our necks. It felt good for awhile but soon the steam from the rag would cook our skin. It seemed to take us forever to get this scything and hoeing done.

Effie Mae and Aunt Sukie brought us something to eat, and we took a long break. We sat down under an oak tree and rested while our stomachs did the same. "Cain't be a werkin' with a bloated belly. Ya mite be a heavin', iffen ya do! Th ol' sun beatin' down on a full belly jist don't ritely mix well," Pa would say.

When we had rested for a spell, we picked up our tools and began the torture all over again. We finally got the garden spot ready for the plowing. Picking up the basket and tools, we headed for the barn. Pa got the plow down from the rafters while I put the harness on old Joker. I stuck the bit in Joker's mouth, gently poked his ears through the crown piece, flattened down the nosepiece, made sure the blinders were straight, and fastened it around his neck. Pa took it from there. He finished putting Joker in the harness and attached the plow. He was ready to plow!

I led Joker to the garden while Pa guided the plow. When we got there, Pa stepped inside a strap, slipped it up around his waist, took the reins, wrapped a rein around each hand and grabbed the plow handles. With a flick of the reins, old Joker began pulling the plow's big wide blade. I don't know if Joker was pulling or Pa was pushing the plow. The plow had a one-sided, curved blade and pitched the soil to the right, leaving a deep rut. Furrows were forming! It wouldn't be long before seed could be sown.

Just as Pa was finishing plowing, old Joker began to get edgy. Even with blinders, Joker was jerking sideways and beginning to eesh haw. Something was on the horizon and it wasn't good. The wind began to blow real hard and dust was flying everywhere. Pa managed to get Joker back to the barn, take off the harness, and lock the corral gate before Joker began to kick.

Looking up to the sky, we saw clouds forming in the southwest. Part of the clouds cast a greenish tinge and were low to the ground. Others were black! Pa yelled for me to fetch all the critters and shut them up in the barn. I didn't have very much trouble. The critters were ready to head for cover and so was I.

About that time, Grammaw, Grampaw, Tut and Baby Jo were coming down the lane real fast. Grampaw had the wagon at full speed as the horse and wagon wheels made dust whirl through the air. As they reached the front door, Grampaw pulled hard on the reins, jerking the wagon and horse to a halt. Grammaw held Baby Jo real tight and ran into the house with Ma and the girls. Tut and Grampaw took the wagon to the barn while Pa and I hurriedly took the harness from the horse.

The wind was blowing really fierce. Small tree limbs and leaves were flying through the air as lightening crashed through the sky. With every lightening flash, you could see a big wall of black descending upon the hills. Thunder rolled so hard, it echoed up the holler. We managed to get back to the house before the rain began to fall. Then the rain stopped as quickly as it started! The silence was eerie. You could feel cold air and hot air at the same time. Winds began to howl and whistle through the trees. In the distance you could hear the sound of trees cracking and smashing to the ground. A roar, a loud beckoning roar, jolted all of us. It sounded like a train coming through the house. Hail started pelting the ground. Some of the hail was as big as a quarter and fell to the ground with a vengeance. The sound was deafening! Then rain began falling so hard you could hear it pour off the mountainside. All of a sudden, it all stopped! It stopped as quickly as it started.

Pa and Grampaw had been covering all of us with their bodies. I do not know how we wound up with quilts over our heads, but we were all crouched together in a corner of the bedroom. There was too much confusion and fear. We cautiously untangled our bodies. One by one, we ventured to look outside. It was a mess! Tree limbs were blown all over the freshly plowed garden, and part of the outhouse was gone. Everything else appeared to be okay. The door on the chicken pen had been blown open and the chickens were loose, but that was a minor inconvenience. At least we were all alive!

Grampaw, Grammaw, Tut and Baby Jo stayed awhile and headed back home. Grampaw told Pa if there was too much damage to the home place, they'd be back for the night. If not, Grampaw would blow the "cow horn."

Pa patted me on the head and said, "Well, J. D., I reckon we done a fair day's werk, but th' storm dun brung us a blessin'. See all them trees, yonder, layin' in th' field? God put'em thar jist fer us. He knowed we needed ta lay by th' wood. I reckon He jist gave us a head start. Better rub sum butter on yer blisters, find ye a clean sock, say yer prayers and git a good nite's rest. Got a lotta werk un a lot a sawin' ta do come mornin'."

"Okay, Pa."

As I was stretched out in bed, thinking about the day and all its glory, being scared of nature's wrath, feeling the blisters pooched out on my hands and being ever so tired, I was calmed by what I heard Ma tell Pa. She said, "Ya know, Pa, we always think we're in control, but I reckon today, God wus tellin' us ta take a better look. We been blessed ever sa much. We still got th' kids, each other, and Grammaw, Grampaw, Tut and Baby Jo. Th' house wus spared frum the winds un we outta be a thank'n th' good Lord thet He wus in control. Th' rainbow after th' storm wus a site ta see, Pa, all them colors painted by God arching across th' sky wus th' sure sign ta have faith in Him."

Ma was right. We had been blessed in so many ways and were lucky to be alive. Then I thought about all the trees and limbs lying about all over the freshly plowed garden spot. Right before I fell asleep, I said, "Thank ya God fer bein in control, but did ya have ta blow down so many dad blamed trees…"

When Daddy had finished his story, all the elderly people began clapping. "You tell'em J. D.; that's the way it was, alright!"

"Why, I remember having blisters. Blisters on top of blisters."

"He was lucky to have a mule. All we had was a hoe!"

"Did he say it rained last night? I don't remember it raining."

Some of the gentlemen were shaking Daddy's hand and thanking him for the story, while others were reminiscing of years long ago. Some had been crying. I hadn't realized the magnitude of effects that one single story could cause, from tears to elation.

It was visible to me that Daddy was really tired. Sitting in the chair for so long had not made his disposition very sunny. He was used to lying in bed as he told me stories and insisted, "Get me back to my bed! My butt feels like it's pinched up around my brain. I am not going to sit like that anymore. If anyone wants to hear these stories, you can tell 'em!"

I took Daddy back to his room, soothed his disposition, kissed him on the forehead and told him I would see him tomorrow. As I walked out of his room, he said, "Don't forget your pencil and paper."

Hobo Cave

For the life of me, I can't figure out how we were always getting into trouble. We didn't go looking for trouble, but if trouble was to be found, we were in the midst of it! Grampaw had told all of us kids about railroad spikes. They were real long. Long enough to be driven through the metal rail and embed deeply into the ground. Some of them even had numbers on the nail head.

We decided to spend some time looking for spikes. We wanted to use them to make a flying ginnie. Since the spikes were real long, they would go through a plank and into a tree stump without any difficulty. When the wind blew, the flying ginnie would spin around. It wasn't much of a toy but it was fun to watch.

We asked Ma and Pa if we could spend the night camped out up in Hobo Cave, near the railroad tracks. They thought about it and said maybe, but to ask Grammaw and Grampaw what they thought about it. Well, we weren't stupid. We told Grammaw and Grampaw that Ma and Pa said it would be okay with them. Effie Mae, Ant Sukie and I could go camping. Then we ran back to my house and told Ma and Pa Tut could go camping. "Cain't we go Ma, please Ma? We'll be real good. We'll behave and not git into trouble."

Ma and Pa finally gave in. "Only if ya promise not ta git in trouble and yer home fer breakfast." It took a lot of flim-flamming to get our way, but we did!

Effie Mae and Aunt Sukie had packed some eating grub in a flour sack and had it flung over their shoulders. Tut and I carried some matches and a couple of quilts. We set off for

Hobo Cave.

We spent most of the afternoon looking for railroad spikes and picked up what we called "treasures." The "treasures" amounted to a flat rock in the shape of a pig, an old rusted horseshoe, colored pebbles, and stogie butts. There were lots of old stogie butts and they sure did stink. We walked up and down the railroad tracks but never did find any spikes, and to top it off, none of the spikes driven into the rails had numbers on them.

Effie Mae said she heard some kind of weird noise but we didn't pay any mind to her. We all heard the noise but we thought it was some kind of critter. Noises in the holler could scare the daylights out you if you were prone to be a skittish sort of person. We weren't skittish; besides, there were four of us. We climbed up the side of the mountain in search of Hobo Cave. We knew it was around there someplace. At last we found the cave. Weeds and brush had grown fairly large and was covering part of the opening. Some of the weeds had been trampled down but we didn't think too much about it. Aunt Sukie pointed to a path and gave us the dickens for not having enough sense to use it. The path led straight up from the railroad tracks. It appeared to have been used quite frequently. Telling her to forget about the path, we slowly went inside the cave. It was dark in there and our eyes had not adjusted to the surroundings. When our eyes adjusted to the dimly lit cave, we realized someone or something had been in the cave just recently. Boy, it was a danged big cave. A whopper!

While Tut and I looked around for some wood to make a campfire, Aunt Sukie and Effie Mae took the grub out of the flour sack. All we had to eat was some cold biscuits and fried smoked hog jowl, but that was all right. For us, that was good eatin'! The campfire was only to keep us warm and the critters away. Tut had scrounged up a pile of wood which had been lying near the back of the cave. Right away, putting a match to it, that old dried wood took fire and began to burn. When the firewood began burning, the smoke drifted upward into the crevices along the top of the cave. Then the smoke started coming down. Lots of danged stinky smoke! We nearly choked to death before we were able to douse it with dirt. We kicked dirt until we thought, "If the smoke don't kill us, the dust will." Deciding we didn't need that big of a fire, we quickly made a smaller campfire. That seemed to do the trick. The smoke was drawing toward the cave opening.

As we began to look around, we found another opening in the long side of the cave. It was a narrow opening and we had to go through it one after the other. There were old burned tin cans with crusted food along the jagged edge of the lid, broken Mason jars, crumpled pieces of paper, and piles of match sticks and stogie butts. Several heaps of grass and leaves had been used for a bed. We weren't willing to go any further into the cave because we thought there might be someone other than us in the cave. It was getting too dark outside to go traipsing home, so knowing we had to be brave, we'd just have to tough out the night.

We finished eating our supper and decided to play some games till we got sleepy. We played king of the mountain. We were hollering and having one devil of a time when Aunt Sukie said she heard a funny noise. The rest of us didn't hear anything, so we didn't pay any attention to her. That girl was always hearing some kind of noise. We just kept on playing. Our playing was cut short in a hurry when we saw flashing lights outside the cave entrance. We fell all over one another as we ran to the entrance trying to find out what or who was causing the lights to flash.

As we looked out of the cave, a crack of thunder just about shook us out of our shoes. We were relieved to know the flashes of light was lightening. The wind began to blow rain inside the cave and we were getting wet. The little campfire was getting wet and we scooted it—the best way we could without getting our hands burned or clothing set a blaze—farther back into the cave.

All of us were getting sleepy and knew the quicker we went to sleep, the quicker we could go home. We pushed all the quilts together and snuggled down for the night. This way we could stay warm, since the rain was making everything really damp. We knew without telling one another this little outing was terrifying. We didn't need to make matters worse by freezing to death. We were just about to lay our heads down when we heard something breathing real hard. The fire had burned down to warm ashes. No flicker of light anywhere. It was pitch tar black! We couldn't see a cockeyed thing, but knew, by George, we weren't alone. The breathing was in front of us and beside us. Breathing was everywhere. Somebody was breathing hard and smoking old stogies, blowing that stinking cigar smoke right in our faces. Phew! It began stinking up the air.

Tut was squashed between me and Aunt Sukie and began to gouge her with his bony old elbows. Effie Mae was gagging for fresh air and started to sneeze.

Pretty soon one of those somebodys said, "Gus, ye better drank some of thet hooch so ye'll stop thet sneezin' or ya mite catch newmonie. I don't wanna be hoppin' thet train without ya."

Gus said, "It ain't me a sneezin', Louie. I reckoned it wus you!"

That's when both of them struck matches and lit up our little corner of the world. Boy, oh boy, we were eyeball to eyeball with two real live hobos. They were looking down at us with squinty eyes, huffing and puffing that smoke out of their nostrils like a dragon. They were some kind of nightmare. They had flung a fear on all four of us. We had heard wild tales about hobos and thought they would tie us up or kill us for sure. I was thinking, "We're in this mess 'cause we wanted ta make a danged old flying ginnie!"

One of the men reached down and patted Effie Mae on the top of her head and said, "Lookie here, Louie, this lil' gal shore nuff looks like yore lil' gal, Sarie Lou."

The man named Louie looked at Effie Mae and started to cry. It was a pitiful sight. We were scared to death of them and they were the ones crying! Louie sat down and had the saddest look on his face. Effie Mae got up from the quilt and slowly walked toward Louie.

Effie Mae was the gentlest female I ever did see. She reached over and patted Louie's knee. "There, there, Mr. Louie. It's gonna be okay. I ain't Sarie Lou but iffen ya stop cryin' ya can call me Sarie Lou."

That's when Mr. Louie started talking about his little girl. She died when she was nine years old. The fever took his beloved wife and only child. That's why he took to the tracks. He was trying to forget what he had lost. He reached inside his worn-out jacket, took out a tattered picture from his pocket and showed the picture to us. We could barely see the picture because it was so dark. Since we didn't have enough light from the matches, Gus gathered up some wood we hadn't used and lit it. Sure enough, Effie Mae was almost a lookalike for Sarie Lou.

Gus began to tell about his family. He had a beautiful red-haired wife and a son, but times were hard, and he couldn't take care of his family the way a man should. He got scared and took to the rails. He wanted to go back home but was afraid he wouldn't be accepted. Besides, he wasn't sure they would still be there if he did.

Those two men were so sad, it made us all cry. We tried to tell them that everybody in the Crossin' would pitch in and try to help them get back on their feet. They understood we were not wealthy with money but were truly rich with love. Tut told them about Ma and Pa loving him like a son and doing everything they could after his Ma died.

We saw the daylight peeking through the opening of the cave. We had talked all night. Convincing Louie and Gus to come home with us, we picked up our quilts and headed home. Ma and Pa were waiting on us. They knew it was time for us to be there but had no idea we would be bringing home hobos. We introduced Louie and Gus to Ma and Pa. They talked for the longest time about circumstances and how to remedy their troubles. They ate breakfast with us and were enjoying all the togetherness when the lonesome old train whistle began blowing.

"Well," they said, "it's time fer us ta leave. Th' whistle is a blowin'. Thank ye rite kindly fer th' food and bein' so kind and lovin' toards us." Then they were gone.

I said, "Pa, th' hobos ain't bad folk. Thay'us jist a mite mixed up. Why cain't thay stay put un build a family like us? Why do thay have ta keep movin' on?"

Giving all us kids a big hug, he said, "Well, thay're searchin' fer thangs whuts in thar own back yard. Thay cain't see th' forest fer th' trees. Thay jist cain't see it!"

We didn't really understand what Pa meant, but Louie and Gus did.

School

You asked me if we ever went to school. Sure, we went to school, but schools back then weren't like they are today. One of the old buildings that belonged to the railroad had been torn down and the wood was going to be thrown away. Instead of getting rid of the wood, an old lady that lived in the holler decided it should be used for a school. She talked Pa and other men into rebuilding it to accommodate kids from the holler. She would be the teacher!

The old building looked okay but it was pretty small. There were about eight classes of kids poked into one room. We didn't have desks or chairs. All we had was a long bench and a table. Some of the older boys whose legs were extremely long would have to sit sideways at the end of the bench. You might not see the same kids more than three times a week, either. Most of the kids would have to help around the house and just didn't show up for school. We also didn't have books or writing paper. You paid attention to what was being said and whether it was right or wrong, learned from what you heard. We learned our ABC's, some math, spelling and how to read by phonics.

Well, I don't mind telling you, but going to school was the "dreaded" time of the year. Not because we needed to learn, but because of the old school marm. She was the most cantankerous, stick-whacking, grouchy old prune-faced woman that ever crawled from a book. I swear that woman had eyes in the back of her head, hands, feet and toes. She also could tell what you were going to say before anything ever came out of your mouth. Somehow she could be at the front of the school and before you knew it, she was looking over your shoulder and making a funny whistling sound through her teeth. It sounded like someone's scraping fingernails down a chalkboard. Her teeth not only made a whistling sound but clacked together if she got real mad. Goosebumps slid down your skin and the roof of your mouth would crawl. She was a mean old biddy and scared the hell out of us kids. I think that old woman practiced how to be mean.

I don't know what circumstances brought her to the holler or what kind of education she had to teach, but between the two of us, you can bet there was never a dull moment. It was as though we both had a strange hold on one another and both of us were bound and determined to have our own way.

We always had to crawl out of bed bright and early, since there were chores to do before we could head off to school. One morning after we had gotten our chores completed, we headed down the lane. The girls went on to the schoolhouse while I waited for Tut down by the creek. We poked around the creek bank, skipping rocks across the water and turning over rocks hunting for critters. We found a few crawdads, scooped up some water in a rusted can and poked them inside, closing the partially opened lid. Then we walked over to the railroad tracks, put our ears down on the rails and listened for the old train. Since we didn't hear a rumble or feel any vibrations, we figured we'd better get on over to school. We couldn't have wasted too much time poking around because the train whistle usually blew about the time school was to start. How wrong we were!

Setting our tin can full of crawdads beside the front door, we proceeded to walk in the door. There stood that old school marm, a hand on one hip, the other hand behind her back. She was stamping her right foot while fire shot out of her eyes. As Tut and I walked past her to sit down, we smiled and said, "Mornin'." She gave a wincing smirking grin telling us we were late, jerked her left hand from around her back and whacked the dickens out of our butts with a stick she fondly called "Mr. Whack," the kindly old gentleman, her "Board of Education" provider.

Tut and I gingerly sat down. Before I realized what I was saying, the words came pouring out of my mouth: "Thet old Bainty Hen dun wacked me fer th' last time. She's jist a mite too free with thet thang. Iffen she whacks me one more time, I reckon I jist mite tell her ta go lay an aigg!" I raised my arms half way up in the air and began flapping them saying, "Clukk, clukk, clukk, barrkk, barrak, clukk, clukk, clukk!"

Then she said quite properly, her teeth clap clacking with every word, "Now, if Mr. Know-It-All can refrain from sounding like a half-grown rooster, we'll get down to business!" With that, she sat down and began to analyze the way I spoke.

She began, "Let's start with phonics. Does anyone know the meaning of phonics?"

There was silence until I said, "Yup! Shore do. It's a body havin' a fondness fer ticks! Don't ritely unnerstand why a body would have a fondness fer ticks. Them old thangs stik thar haids in yer skin un draw out yer blud! Thay make ya itch too."

You could see the school marm shoot smoke out of her ears. Something was surely making her mad cause she was shaking her head side to side, sucking air through her teeth. "NO! It ain't, I mean, isn't a fondness fer, uh, for ticks. Phonics means relating to sounds of words. Such as the word THEY. How do you suppose that word spells?"

I piped up again: "T-H-E-T."

"What is T-H-E-T?"

"It's thet word ya wanted spelt. Ya jist said how do you suppose thet word is spelt!"

"Thet is no such word! They, spell THEY!"

"T-H-A-Y!"

"NO! The correct spelling is, T-H-E-Y."

"Mam, if yore fondness fer ticks makes THAY spelt T-H-E-Y, then I'm a monkeys uncle. Everbody knows thet THE 'Y' means th' why of somethin'."

The school marm said, "Let's get on to something else. Someone please spell woodchuck." All the kids looked at one another and made attempts to spell the word woodchuck. After awhile when no one spelled it correctly, I raised my hand. I wasn't sure she would allow me to open my mouth, but she reluctantly told me to go ahead.

I thought for a minute and spelled, "Whud whittle tis whud, tis chuckin der chuck, whud whittle be whud, C- h- u- c- k!" Instead of stopping right then, I continued, "How much wood could a woodchuck chuck if a woodchuck could chuck wood?"

The school marm yelled, "Everyone outside. Get some fresh air!" After a few minutes, she yelled for us to come back in the schoolhouse. She apparently had calmed down. While we were playing, I noticed her standing just outside the front door. She had been tidying the schoolyard, picking up sticks and piling them neatly beside the rock stoop. She reached down and picked up my tin can. She shook it, realized there was water inside, held the top of the lid down and poured the water out.

As we filed in and took our seats, I saw the tin can sitting on the front table. I jabbed Tut in the ribs and pointed. We could see the crawdads' antennae and a claw sticking out the jagged tin lid.

The marm sat down in her chair. "Now children," she began, "we won't continue spelling. Let's turn to numbers." All of us stated aloud: "One plus one equals two, two plus two equals four," and continued our numbers until we reached ten plus ten equals twenty. I raised my hand to ask her if she could answer a question about numbers.

"Of course I can. Ask me a question."

"Iffen a hen and a half can lay an aigg and a half in a day

and a half, how many aiggs or brass doorknobs can a rooster lay in one day?"

She sat there with the dumbest look on her face. She got up from her chair, walked around with her left hand on her hip and her right hand resting on her cheekbone. She was thinking really hard. A few minutes lapsed as she sat back down in her chair saying, "You know, J. D., you've asked a very hard question but good question. It appears that I do not know the answer. Will you please tell the answer to all of us?"

Everyone broke into laughter when I said, "Well, it's like this. Roosters can't lay aiggs and iffen it could lay a brass doorknob, we'd shore nuff be dumbfounded!"

All of a sudden, she let out a scream that just about deafened all of us and began fanning her hands in circles; her arm went sideways and the tin can went flying across the room. Crawdads were everywhere, girls were squealing and the marm was dancing all over the place. One of the crawdads had crawled up her old brown stockings, got hung in a wrinkle and couldn't get free. That's the day hell broke loose in the schoolhouse.

Since none of us could get our minds on learning, she said, "All of you go home! I don't want to see any of you until next week."

Well, that morning went over like a ton of bricks. I knew that when I got home another ton of bricks would be heading my way. All sorts of things were running through my head. I figured after the girls told Ma what happened I'd get the tar wailed out of me.

Ma took me aside and said, "J. D., when ya opened th' book, did ya read th' first page of th' first chapter or did ya skip to th' last page?"

"Whut book?"

"Ya ponder 'bout it fer awhile, okay?"

That night, I lay awake thinking about what Ma said. It

dawned on me what Ma's one-liner meant. The first page tells a beginning, the middle explains the reason for the first page and the last page brings everything together. Everybody in this world has a job to do and if you don't take the time to learn the meaning and reasoning behind the job, you won't be successful. Not only that, I hadn't gotten past the first page of her personality to appreciate her love for learning, so she could pass along what she had learned to help us succeed in life.

After swallowing my pride, the next week...I took her flowers.

Snuff

Remember me telling you about Grampaw's love for chawin "terbakkie" and pipe terbakkie and Grammaw's fondness for snuff?

Well, Tut and I decided to try our hand at spitting. We practiced with water but all that did was make us wet, and besides, it sprayed too much. Then we tried to spit cucumber seeds. That didn't work because they were too slimy. We finally settled on pumpkin seeds. Pumpkin seeds were just the right size of a good wad of chawin' "terbakkie" or lip full of snuff. Only thing, though: it didn't leave a brown stain. Getting tired of spitting pumpkin seeds, we decided to try to smoke a pipe. Grampaw always had four or five old pipes lying around and wouldn't miss two of them, since he was always laying them down in odd places.

We knew if we snitched his pipe terbakkie from the little cotton pouch, he'd find out. He always folded the pouch in half, wrapped twine around the middle and tied it in a weird knot. He called it the "in a hurry knot." All he had to do was pull one of the strings and the knot came out. Trouble is, we didn't know which string to pull. We settled on wild muskedine leaves.

Each of us sneaked a corn cob pipe and three matches and shoved them under our armpits. If Grampaw or Grammaw asked us what we had in our pockets, we could truthfully say "nothin'." We left Tut's house and walked down the path toward the Crossin'. Instead of going to my house, we headed for the muskedine vines.

Muskedine leaves are real large, like grape leaves. That's

because muskedines and tame grapes are in the same family. Since you can eat the muskedines and grapes, we thought the leaves would be safe as well. We pulled a few green leaves off the vine, wadded them up in our hand and shoved them into the corncob pipe bowl. We put a lighted match to it and sucked real hard on the pipe stem. Not a cockeyed thing! No smoke! A gosh awful smell, but no smoke. The smell was enough to choke a horse. It smelled like old rags burning.

We knew we were doing something wrong but didn't realize what it was until I looked at Tut and saw the front of his britches smoking. He had stuck the match inside his pocket. The head of the match was still hot and had burned a hole the size of a marble straight through those old wool britches. Wool does not burn like cotton. Cotton goes up in a puff of glory but wool has a tendency to melt and gets harder than concrete around the melted edges. We had to do some powerful thinking as to how to explain the hole in his trousers, but we'd think about that later. We wanted to find something to poke in those pipes.

We sat down on the ground trying to decide what would burn like terbakkie. We looked around but everything was too green. What we needed was…a light bulb went off in our heads at the same time. Dried up old corn shucks or hay! We got up and raced as fast as we could to the barn. We knew Pa had stored a tent of corn shucks for outhouse purposes. Reaching the barn, we ran to the corner where the corn shucks were curing. We quickly grabbed up several hands full of corn shucks and hay and shoved them inside our pockets. Then we hurriedly headed back to the creek bank.

At last we could find out why Grampaw enjoyed smoking the terbakkie. We decided to use the hay first. The hay was really dry and because some of the hay blades were hollow, we figured it would be the easiest to smoke. We packed our pipes as tight as we could get them. Some of the hay was sticking up too far above the pipe rims, but when it started burning, it would soon look like Grampaw's terbakkie: Nice and smooth with a whisper of smoke.

We only snitched three matches, and because we wanted to try the corn shucks, this second match had better make the hay catch fire. Placing the pipes in our mouths, we put our heads close together and Tut struck the match. As the fire hit the hay and we took a long breath, the hay ignited and exploded into a ball of fire. Pooof! Pieces of hay were floating up in the air in a blackened rage, curling up into bits and pieces and falling to the ground. Standing up as quickly as we could, we began to stamp the ground, putting out embers of blackened hay and slapping at our clothing. We looked at one another and began to laugh. The front of our hair had been singed and we didn't have any eyebrows.

Now we had three problems: How to explain the hole in Tut's britches, why we didn't have any eyebrows and how the front of our hair became so blunt.

There was only one match left. Were we going to use it or not? Thinking about it for awhile and knowing if we didn't try the corn shucks, we'd regret it, we took some of the shredded corn shucks, wound them around and around to make a little ball, and put them in the pipes. We packed it in real tight and lit the pipes, knowing if we weren't careful, we might be jumping in the creek. We couldn't afford for anything else to catch on fire. Taking a big draw on the pipes, we found the pipes and the contents not very favorable.

Breathing in the first draw wasn't so bad. It was the second, third and fourth. The first draw was like walking through smoke drifting down toward the ground from a chimney. The second draw had a bit of a bite to the tongue and made a bad taste in the mouth. The third draw was not any better than the first or second, simply because we hadn't inhaled any of the smoke. The fourth draw was a lulu! As we took in a big, deep, inhaling breath, the fire from smoldering pipe shot up through the pipe stem and burned like hell. Smoke was coming out of our mouths and noses. We began to cough real hard but the smoke seemed to go down further inside our lungs with every gulp of air.

We tried to stand up but couldn't get a foothold on the ground. We were dizzy, weak-kneed, felt the diarrhea surge through our guts and knew any minute, both of us would start to puke. We coughed and gagged until tears were coming out of our eyes. We stayed on the ground for a very long time before we made the decision not to try that anymore. It was dangerous as hell!

Gathering our wits, we picked ourselves off the ground and headed to Tut's house to put the pipes back where we found them. We had just sneaked them back when Grammaw yelled for us to go to Mr. Matlock's store. She wanted us to get a small tin of snuff for her. The tin of snuff was probably an inch in diameter and one and one half inches high. A paper seal was secured from the top of the lid down over the container.

We walked to the store, bought the snuff for Grammaw and proceeded to go back up the hill. Halfway up the hill we decided to try dipping the snuff. Dummy us! We hadn't given much thought to breaking the seal or that when we broke the seal, Grammaw would know right away what we had done. Dipping our little finger in the snuff, we gouged out a bit of snuff and shoved it under our front lip. Nothing to it! Piece of cake! That is, until the snuff began to get wet with spit. The snuff began to liquefy and swell inside our mouths, making wads of spit form faster than we could bear. The sickening sweet taste started the diarrhea surge all over again. We were frothing at the gills and white as a sheet! All the color had drained from our faces; dirty brown rings had formed around our mouths; our teeth were a shade of brownish green ick and we couldn't get the snuff off the inside of our lips. It was stuck like glue and burned like fire.

We held on to one another as we walked up that hill. The more we walked, the steeper the hill got. It was as though the hill wouldn't quit. We could see the house, but at the same time, it got farther away. Finally we got to the front stoop. Grammaw wanted to know what took so long and why we looked like something the cats wouldn't bury. She also wanted to know how the seal was broken. Tut said it accidentally dropped it on a sharp rock. Grammaw said if we were lying, our tongues would swell up with sharp, pointed, spit-raising lie bumps.

Well, this was one day to remember. Tut had a hole in his britches, part of our hair was singed to the scalp, we had no eyebrows, Grampaw's pipes were black as coal, we stunk to high heaven, we were sicker than junkyard dogs, our teeth were green and our tongues were brown, and to top it off, Grammaw knew we were lying. Another thing we had to contend with was those spit-raising lie bumps across the end of our tongues that we always got when we told a fib or an out and out lie. Although Grammaw knew we had dipped snuff, she only said three words…check your tongues! She just grinned real big and walked away.

Surprise! It's the Halloween "Swamp Baby"

Halloween was a fun time for all of us. Maybe it was because I was born on Halloween, or perhaps it was because we were able to have a hoe-down in the barn with all the hill folks. Anyway, one Halloween I can remember was more than anyone bargained for or wanted to repeat.

This particular Halloween was set aside for a barn dance or hoe-down, or whatever you want to call it. All the hill folk came together to rejoice in their fortune for having good crops and to have a good time playing music on their fiddles, banjos, spoons, jugs, harmonicas or whatever instrument they had available. It didn't matter what the instruments were made of but how the music sounded when they all got together.

Pa would clean out a portion of the barn, pile hay along the side walls of the barn for sitting and scrape the floor for an area to dance. All of us would pitch in and help decorate the rafters. It wasn't any easy task but somehow we managed to hang streamers made out of old strips of cloth with big balls of papier-mâché dangling on the ends. The papier-mâché balls were made from old newspapers being torn into strips, flour-glued together and then wadded into odd shapes. After the balls dried, Grammaw would dip them into a solution of water and dried pokeberries.

Pokeberries are the bright purple seeds from "poke greens," which only grow in the spring. We'd eat the tender poke greens and when the poke went to seed, Grammaw would collect the berries, dry them and then use them for dye. Anyway, all the papier-mâché balls turned a light shade of purple and looked real pretty hanging from the rafters, but the light from the coal oil lanterns made eerie shaped shadows dance on the dirt floor. It really gave me the creeps!

Around dusk everyone from miles around would begin to arrive in the horse-drawn buggies, unload the family, instruments and food they brought and assemble in the barn for the festivities. Most of the men would gather in one area, the women in another and all of us kids would convene in a group to play games until we were tired and then sit in a huddle to tell tall tales of apparition stories. In other words, spooky ghost stories!

Before long the barn was alive with music, singing and dancing. The hillside was set afire with sounds bouncing off trees. It was as though the hills were dancing and enjoying the delightful sounds of happy people, wanting to embrace every note of enthusiastic rhythm. Dried leaves being blown from the trees swirled to the ground, encircling each other in square dance form. As the music subsided, the leaves calmly drifted to their resting place as though they were tired from a marathon dance. Everything and everyone was touched that evening with harmonious spirits.

All of us kids, maybe fifty or so, had tired of bobbing our heads into a washtub filled with apples and water. Each one of us would take turns, trying desperately to bite an apple floating in water. It seemed like such a simple procedure, but holding your breath with your mouth wide open in an attempt to retrieve an apple was not as easy as expected. As the face hits the cold water, the eyes automatically shut, the nose tries to breathe and water shoots up through the eyes and down the throat. It would shock the senses and nearly choke you to death by releasing waves of sputtering coughs. Trying to stop the coughing merely made the water shoot up through the nose. That's one terrible sensation!

We were sopping wet and getting cold. Luckily Pa had built an in-ground campfire with rocks piled all around the open flame area, and we delighted in standing near the exuding warmth. After we each had a go at bobbing for the apples, we reached in the tub, took out an apple and sat down in a circle around the campfire. It was time to begin our ghostly resurrection.

A lot of stories were told, and they did give us goosebumps and made our hair stand on end. With each story told, we all scooted closer to the fire. Maybe it was to stay warm, but I had a sneaking suspicion that it was because fear was closing in on us and the fire gave us added protection from what went bump in the night.

It finally came my time to tell a ghost story. I wasn't sure how to begin my story but with a little bit of thought I began to evoke a hair-raising tale that sent us into screaming fits. I began…

"It all started in th' summer of 1832. Thar was this woman who lived in th' snaky 'n gater swamps near th' river. It's been told thet she had a family but somethin' happened to'em. Nary a soul knoed whut happened but it seemed they jist disappeared. It twern't wise fer people ta poke inta her bisness cause iffen thay did, bad thangs would befall upon'em.

"People whut saw her durin' th' day, said she looked like a shrived old hag and laughed like a banshee iffen she saw someone comin'. Thet old woman was a fearful sight! Her hair was matted together in long strings, almost down ta her waist. She would run toard th' river bank tryin' ta grab th' people who were poachin' in her territory. Her fingers looked like long, pointy twigs as she tried ta clinch her fists in a panicked rage. It was known fer sure she was some kinda witch 'n had a power over th' swamp.

"Ever now 'n then, by th' lite of th' moon, men whut was lookin' fer gaters would very quietly float thar boats inta th' swamps. Wiff thar coal oil lanters perched on th' small seats of th' boat, th' lantern would commence ta flicker long shadows against th' water. It cast an eerie glow whut made th' trees glare as though thay had eyes black as coal tar silt. Th' wind would blow th' tangled moss 'n limbs as if th' trees were tryin' ta whisper thar deep dark secrets. Nite time was th' hour fer fear! Thar twern't much ta look at durin' th' day but come nite fall, th' trees would plunge th' lite inta deep black darkness 'n th' big gnarly tree roots hangin' 'n reachin' down inta th' river beckoned fer souls ta come closer. Big pieces of moss hung frum th' tree limbs whilst th' snakes slithered 'n coiled around th' large muscled tree limbs. Th' trees jist seemed ta' grow 'n spread faster 'n faster. It was as though thay were jist watchin 'n waitin.

"Well, early one morning, three men figgered ta search th' swamp fer some of thar friends whut never come out of th' swamp. Thay drifted up near th' bank not makin' a sound. Slowly, one by one thay inched thar way outta th' boat 'n onta th' soggy ground. As thay crept through th' mushy water 'n soil one of th' men stepped onna big piece of wood. He realized he was steppin' on part of a small boat. As he began ta move th' boat wiff his hand, more rotted boats began ta come ta th' surface. Thar was dozens of'em! As he started ta yell fer his two friends, th' old woman lookin' down at him frum a big tree, commenced ta laugh inna high-pitched wail. She said, 'Thar's one, honey, git him!' Th' massive tree where she was sittin' raised th' large gnarly root 'n sucked him under th' tree.

"Th' other two men watched in horror as th' tree shook 'n grew bigger 'n bigger. Th' old woman was heard to say as she patted the tree, 'Thet's my baby. Yore a good baby! Rock a bye baby in th' tree top. Thay tried ta tell me you were dead but I knoed! I knoed thet ya was still breathin'. I warned'em not ta put thet dirt over ya 'n not ta plant no tree. Thay said I was crazy but I ain't crazy. I knoed ya would live fer ever cause I been feedin' ya rite good! I showed'em! All them people whut covered ya up, made ya grow rite fast. It fed ya real good! Jist wait, baby, another body will lean up against your trunk 'n you can reach out and…GRAB'EM!'"

About the time I finished telling my ghost story, all of us kids noticed the fire had died down and we were getting cold. It had gotten darker and only a flicker of light was coming from the coals. As I stood up to go get Pa to add more wood to the fire, I noticed it was pitch black all around us. The barn door was closed and panic shot through my stomach. Where did everyone go? All of a sudden, we all heard a high-pitched screaming from what we thought was the old banshee woman. I let out a blood-curdling scream, and pandemonium began.

Effie Mae and Aunt Sukie were the first to go berserk! When they started screaming, all the other girls began to scream. Then all the boys went into a tail spin. Tut was trying to stutter a few unintelligible curse words and trying to crawl toward the barn. Panic had reached an all-time high. Dirt was flying everywhere from feet-gouging footholds in a scramble to vacate the premises, and half-chewed yellowed apple cores came soaring through the air like low-launched ground to air missiles.

While we were engrossed in telling ghost stories, we had not noticed the background activities emerging around us. Pa, Grampaw and all the other daddies had been listening to the tale of "Swamp Baby" and decided to have a little fun.

They had poked corn shucks over their heads and down around their trousers. Tree limbs were crammed up their long shirtsleeves with the ends of the branches dangling down toward the ground. They were standing within two inches of our backs. Before we knew what happened, the tree branches were tapping us on the shoulders and trying to grab us. When our eyes adjusted to seeing the "trees" standing behind us and hearing "Rock A Bye Baby" being sung in such low voices and the "trees" saying, "Grab'em," kids flew like terrified jackrabbits in all directions. It scared the living hell out of us!

It took me a long time before I wanted to hear "Rock A Bye Baby" again and even longer to get me to scoot up next to a tree trunk. Even though it was a simple ghost story, "Swamp Baby" was alive and well on that spooky Halloween night.

Ye Gods! Sweetaters, Greens and Persimmons

About the middle of August, the persimmon trees would hail forth an abundance of small, hard, perfectly round, green formations of the persimmon fruit. If the weather was just right, in just a few short weeks the fruit would soon blossom into the brightest orange, sweet-tasting, delicate mouth poppers you could imagine. All of us kids delighted in the fact that we could begin the ritual of our yearly "get-together" for the bombardment of persimmon splat smackers.

Rule number one was that any persimmon had to be fully ripe, free of any twigs hanging onto the fruit and absolutely no substitution of any hard object. It couldn't be a facsimile. In other words, no cock-eyed rocks!

Rule number two was that the persimmons could not be projected unless "airborne" or "incoming" was announced with a vigorous yell. It was the duty of the captain on each team to make sure his troops didn't wind up with a black eye or a pump knot on the head. Of course, we all managed to sling a few persimmons without the usual announcements and that made the persimmon fights even more comical because they always landed with great precision right on someone's backside or skimmed the scalp. When that happened, your hair would goop up and become slimy with persimmon seeds stuck in all directions.

Rule number three was that the launching mechanism could not be any longer than two and one half feet and the circumference no larger than the index finger. In other words, don't use a big stick! That might have been okay except that some of the kids' index fingers were larger than their fighting buddy.

Rule number four was that if anyone yelled "time out," everyone had to lay down his ammunitions and wait until the captains said to commence firing. It seemed to me that "time out" shouldn't be a part of this battle since real wartime battles didn't have any "time outs." Anyway, we adhered to the rules because if we didn't, it was sure that someone would go tattling. That someone was a rotten old sister hanging around where she didn't need to be hanging around. The girls didn't want to participate in the persimmon fights but they sure liked causing trouble.

Rule number five was merely to eat as many persimmons as your gut could hold without becoming green around the gills. I don't mind telling you that too many persimmons had the ability to turn the stomach inside out and send a body scampering behind the nearest large tree. Believe me, there's something in persimmons kin to a laxative! Lucky for us, we were only able to eat persimmons after the persimmon fight. Trouble was, all of us ate more than we should.

It was fun sitting there in the midst of all those big strapping boys perched upon boulders, looking at each other with persimmon slime hanging on to every strand of hair, clothes all mushy with pulp, faces tinged a light shade of orange, teeth crunching through the mellow flesh of fruit and spitting with great gusto the large oval seeds as far as a big breath of air would send them. Every now and then, if we weren't careful, a seed would successfully find its way down our throats and send us all gagging. It wasn't because it was a seed but because it was slippery and felt like a big hawker sliding down the back of the throat from blobs of snot being dislodged from a stuffed-up nose or from someone clearing his throat from a nasty post nasal drip.

After we sat there stuffing our faces and guts with the yellow laxatives, we began to cut open the seeds. Not many of us had knives but those who did would carefully rub the seeds into the dirt to remove any excess slime, stick the pointed edge into the tip of the seed and slowly chisel into the hard outer coating of the seed. It took a bit of doing because as hard as we tried, the seed would somehow shoot through the fingertips and land in the bushes. After a cautious search...we didn't know if the seed was actually in the bushes or if a sneaky snake was waiting to lay a bite on an unsuspecting arm or leg...we might find the seed in question. Usually the seed would be elusive and we would have to start all over. When we finally did pry open a seed, the most fascinating surprise would be waiting for us.

Inside the seed was the most unusual formation of a perfectly-formed knife, a three-tined fork and spoon. Sometimes there would only be a spoon or a fork, or maybe a knife and fork or a combination of two of the three eating utensils. The grownups used to say the combination of utensils indicated the severity of winter weather. Whatever the case, it was a fascinating discovery of how the trees could provide a source of delicate tasty food for humans and critters and entertainment in the way of a free-for-all in a persimmon fight.

After about three hours of fighting, eating and carving, it was time to call it a day. We were all tuckered out from heaving persimmons through the air and knew it was time to head off in the direction of our homes. We headed off toward the house and each of the boys yelled for his sisters to get a move on. It took awhile for the girls to gather their senses and join their brothers, but eventually everyone went to his house knowing that the day was full of fun and hoping to resume the games the following Saturday. That would hinge, however, on the amount of chores each of us had to do.

That afternoon, me and Tut were stretched out in the loft of the barn. We were sicker than junkyard dogs from gorging on persimmons but had to keep it a secret. Ma had already warned us not to eat so many of the dad blamed things but we couldn't tell the rest of the guys that "Ma says not ta be a eatin' them thangs. Yer gonna puke yore guts up, jist like ya did th' last time." We were miserable but somehow would have to pretend the seeds we ingested along with all the fleshy fruit were not the culprit of indigestion or the exudation of aromatic backside perfume. We lay in the barn for at least thirty minutes before Grammaw yelled for us to come eat supper. Ye gods, supper?

Me and Tut looked at one another in great disgust, pursed our lips and gagged. How in thunder would we be able to eat supper? There wasn't an empty spot inside our guts to hold another piece of food, let alone look at food. If we knew what was good for us, we'd choke down that food whether we liked it or not.

We slowly walked to the house, sloshing with every step we took and letting off a few stink bombs. As we walked into the kitchen, a familiar smell nearly knocked us off our feet. We looked at one another and knew right away we were in for big trouble. It was sweet taters and greens! Heavenly days, sweet taters and greens combined with persimmons: that's deadly! We like all three...but not together...not all in one day.

Sweet taters are orange. Persimmons are orange. Greens are green. When you mix those colors together, it makes a bad omen. Worse to come? A race to the outhouse!

Me and Tut sat there picking at our food when Grampaw said, "Them's some rite good lookin' sweet taters. Gimmie thet butter! Ain't nuthin' like pokin' th' butter inta th' steamin' taters. Boy, them greens shore nuff look larapin'. Hummm...th' hog lard makes th' pot 'likker' slurpin' delicious and gives'em a good smell. Boys, ya better gittcha a bite. Ya don't wanna go hungry."

In our haste to squelch the kabooms which gravitated to our backsides, a silent accidental swish of air escaped into the combination of odors hovering around our nostrils. As Grampaw placed a bite of sweet taters near his mouth, he stopped short of eating and looked around the room. By this time everyone could smell the "accident," but no one said a word. After all, sweet taters are notorious for noxious fumes, and everyone had already partaken of the delicate morsel.

Greens, on the other side of the picture, leave a whole lot to be desired. In our short lifetime, we had consumed so many greens that in order to keep standing on both feet, we had to tie a coal-oiled rag around our legs to keep the cut worms from chewing our legs into shards thinking we were a tasty green treat growing in the garden. Fact of the matter, the consumption of any type of greens, stringy or broad-leafed, will wrap around whatever is in its way and squeeze uniformly into the forefront of eau d'stink sulfuric "accidents." It's like a silent auction. No one knows who is doing the highest bidding 'cause they keep their mouths shut and pretend they've been out-bid.

After we all had consumed our evening meal, cleared the table and did our usual chores, it was time for us to gather around in the living room to talk about what we did that day, play some dominoes while it was still light enough to see who was cheating, and listen to Grampaw and Pa play their fiddles. Since it was Saturday, we delighted in getting to stay up later than usual. Grammaw and Grampaw, Tut and Baby Jo were spending the night with us because Pa and Grampaw wanted to get up at first light to scout for the new crop of fallen pecans and hickory nuts.

Grammaw had gone to the kitchen and popped a great big pan full of popcorn. It smelled really good but how in tarnation were we supposed to eat that stuff with all the other "stuff" adhering to the insides of our intestines? There wasn't enough room for the noxious gasses, let alone several kernels of corn piled high on persimmons, sweet taters and greens. It was like adding fuel to the raging inferno about to erupt in me and Tut and heaven help us…Grampaw!

Grampaw, as much as we loved him, could secrete silent but deadly "mistakes." Larger than life he was, and his insides could rock and roll with the best of entertainers. You could actually see his stomach twist and turn and hear the rumbling of the forthcoming sonic boom. It was like watching a wrestling match between two tigers fighting over which one could carry off the largest game, and at the same time anticipating his maneuvers as when to take cover or run to the nearest exit for air.

You never knew about Grampaw. It's not to say that Grampaw was uncouth or crass, but one minute he could be as passive as a baby lamb and the next minute he was hiking his leg, exuding a forceful "mistake" that sent everyone into rigors. Then he would laugh and say, "Whew, thar's more room on th' outside thun whut I got inside my innards." Talk about chemical warfare! Grampaw could have bottled that stuff and sold it to the armed services. After consuming several handfuls of popcorn…the race was on. A race to the outhouse!

Me and Tut had been listening to the fiddles and decided to horse around. As we began wrestling on the floor, a wave of uncontrollable "mistakes" began to nauseate our senses. Pretty soon, our stomachs began to growl and churn like a raging river, making sounds of an impending flood. As we stood up, turned and looked at one another, Tut grabbed his stomach and shot out the back door in a mad race to the outhouse and I was right behind him.

Unfortunately, I was unable to extract myself from the premises as rapidly as I should have. Halfway down the path to the outhouse, I realized all was not well. The pain in my stomach was growing with great intensity and the trap door on my backside was slowly but surely releasing a faint stream of liquid. As soon as I realized the magnitude of my dilemma, I quickly slowed my gait to a knee-knocking movement. Taking a real deep breath, I pressed my knees together and began walking on the insides of my feet, one baby step at a time. Hobbling down the path, knowing I only had around twenty-five feet to go before I could take advantage of the outhouse, Grampaw came up behind me in a full-blown, galloping run. The steed was on the loose and I didn't stand a chance of a snowball in hell beating him to the outhouse.

When I finally reached the outhouse, panic began to surge through my body. When I say surge, I mean surge! Tut was on one side of the outhouse and Grampaw was on the other. I began to pound the doors telling them that one of them needed to get out of there 'cause if they didn't I would be sitting on somebody's lap. It seemed like forever before Tut opened the door. A door which was holding back a mountainous supply of fruitful "mistakes." To say the least, I didn't know which was worse…what I contained or what the outhouse contained.

Stepping in to the outhouse, I tried to take a deep breath of fresh air, knowing at any minute I could be asphyxiated from the "presents" being sent by Grampaw, who was sitting on the other side of the outhouse. Only a thin piece of wood separated us from killing each other!

I heard Grampaw let out a sigh of relief as he shuffled his feet. I knew he was on the way out of the outhouse because he began whistling a tune. That meant he was happy when he exited the outhouse, and I can truthfully say I was happy to know it would finally be silent on the other side of the outhouse.

It was short lived! Before I knew it, Pa was blowing the bottom out of the cubicle vacated by Grampaw and the girls were pounding on my door, letting me know and everyone in the holler that if I knew what was good for me, I'd get off the throne. I was currently in a very bad way and my very existence was threatened with major bodily harm from being in a bad way. I didn't know which was worse: A gut ache or dying! Any way I turned, I was bound to have someone yelling for me to "Git outta thar!"

Something was surely wrong with this family! I know why me and Tut were sicker than junkyard dogs but didn't have one iota as to why the rest of the family was hell-bent for leather to get to the outhouse.

That evening as we all breathed a sigh of relief knowing the treks to the outhouse were possibly over, I found out why everyone, except Ma and Grammaw, was racing en masse to the outhouse.

It wasn't just persimmons, sweet taters, greens and popcorn! It also was homemade apple cider and sorghum molasses cookies and one extra little secretive "something" for an added punch!

I probably would never have known the reason for the exodus to the outhouse if it hadn't been for Ma and Grammaw standing on the front stoop, snickering like two little girls having just seen a three-ring circus clown running amok with an elephant stampede. Ma laughing real hard as she said to Grammaw, "I reckon we jist did a rite good job doin' th' fall cleanin'. Ya knoed whut, Grammaw, it was like takin' candy frum a baby. Shucks, twern't nary no fight holdin' th' nose or droppin' a smidgen bit ta th' floor. Thay didn't knoe whut hit'em!"

"Yup! Damned site easier thun I was thinkin'." Grammaw, laughing almost uncontrollably, said, "Pa needs ta git his smeller fixed. Danged old nut cain't tell th' difference tween hog lard pot likker'n medicinal castor oil!"

Blue Ain't Blue
but Blackie Is Black

During the spring, wonderful and mysterious things seemed to erupt simply by the masterful creations of God. The lifeline for this earth was slowly but surely popping and springing into glorious fruition. It always amazed me how each tree, flower and critter knew the season for production, and what truly sent my mind racing was and is the remarkable way things can live in harmony with just a little bit of love and tenderness.

Let me tell you about Blackie and Blue.

It was early one spring morning. The air was filled with the promise of a day full of surprises and it made the heart leap with anticipation. It's a hard thing to describe but the stomach has a fluttery feeling and the heart is so full of love that you just can't stand being alone. It makes you want to hug your family and tell them how very much they're loved. It's like remembering the first day of school and having the memory of various aromas associated with walking through wet grasses tickling the backside of pant legs. It's a fresh new day waiting to surround the mind and soul.

Anyway, as usual, we all began tending to what needed to be done around the home place. From a distance, the sound of low-slung, flop-eared Beagles and Blue Tick Hounds baying at the sight of rabbits and other critters caught our ears with a joyous and sometimes high-pitched wail.

Beagles and Blue Tick Hounds were notorious for running their legs off in hot pursuit of anything they couldn't catch. Those dogs, as well as other breeds, would lay their noses to the ground, head off for parts unknown and sniff their brains out until they lay exhausted from going around in circles. Grampaw always said, "Them dawgs ain't got no lick of sense. Ya cain't keep'em penned up, thay can dig thar claws through barbed wire fences and tarn thar noses up ta food iffen thay have a mind ta run. Iffin' thay would shut thar mouths 'n quit thar bellowin', thay jist might be able ta sneak up on whut thay're chasin'. Anythang whut thar chasin' hears'em nigh on ta an hour afore thay git whar thay're goin'. Thay jist ain't no rhyme ta reason why anyone would buy one of them critters. Why pay money fer sumthin' thet jist won't stay put!"

Well, today was going to be different. We were not expecting to find anything out of the ordinary, but to our surprise, nature has a way of smacking you in the jaws just when you least expect it.

Effie Mae and Aunt Sukie were in the front yard picking up sticks and various sorts of things to appease Grammaw. Grammaw always said that "Idle hands are the devil's workshop," and she made sure we never had time on our hands to create unsightly messes. She liked a clean environment and intended that we learn how everything coincided for a proper place in structure, especially in our minds and atmosphere surrounding us. Who were we to argue the point with Grammaw?

Out of the clear blue sky came screams from both of the girls. Naturally everyone came running to see if they were hurt or if they were in one of their screaming modes just to rattle our brains. It was neither. They had the beejeebers scared right out of them when Aunt Sukie bent over close to the front stoop and accidentally stepped on the backside and long tail of "Blue." When she unknowingly stepped on the tail, the dog automatically turned its head in her direction. It didn't growl, but did show an unsightly bit of black and white teeth as though it was smiling. However, the teeth weren't black. It was the object clenched between its pearly white teeth.

By this time everyone was crouched around the front porch trying to get a better look at what just adopted us. Grammaw got down on her knees and gently persuaded the dog to come from under the porch. She talked to the dog with such tenderness and finesse that within a few seconds the dog scooted its way out from under the porch and plopped beside Grammaw.

The poor little thing was sure in a mess. Its paws were all torn and crammed with stickers and it had spots where it shouldn't have had spots. When Grammaw saw this poor little dog, so hurt and hungry, we all were transformed into a fast-forward movement. She was yelling out instructions for each of us and we were responding.

Grampaw got the old black salve and coal oil, Ma brought water and hog jowl, Pa had a pan full of wash water, lye soap and rags, and all of us kids were made to sit down and be quiet. Keeping our mouths shut and staying out of the way was worse than being hog-tied. Watching them tend to all the cuts was like watching a masterful surgeon's team in sync. Precision at its best.

Grampaw gently lifted each paw and began to remove splinters from the bruised and cut pads while Pa washed each one very carefully. Ma dipped each paw into coal oil to ward off infections and then rubbed black salve deep into the wounds. Grammaw then wrapped each paw with a piece of cloth to keep the dirt from re-entering the cuts. When that was completed, the dog was picked clean of ticks, scrubbed down to reveal a beautiful white spotted coat of hair, dried thoroughly and then gently laid on a bed of straw. A couple of times the dog tried to get back under the porch as a pitiful look came upon its face as though it was trying to tell us there was something else. Grammaw picked up on the communication and looked beneath the front stoop.

There it was! The object of Blue's affection. Grammaw lifted the poor little thing and cradled it in her hand. She then took it over to Blue and let Blue sniff it a couple of times and then Blue fell asleep. Blue knew his little friend was in safekeeping.

When Grammaw finally uncupped her hands to reveal the little black object, we were surprised to see a fledgling baby crow. It looked like an emaciated budgie! All of the feathers appeared to be bigger than the body and they weren't even fully grown. It seemed as though the wings were cropped off with a pair of scissors but Grammaw assured us that they were still in transition and would soon become beautiful wings. One thing different about this little baby crow was the crippled foot. The foot was not broken but a simple deformity from birth. The little thing either tried to fledge too soon or the mother shoved it from the nest. Whatever the case, Blue, the "bird dog," didn't try to hurt the crow but was merely trying to save it.

We all watched as Grammaw dipped sourdough biscuits into water, tickled the neck of the baby crow to encourage the beak to lift into the air, and then dropped blobs of mushy bread deep into its throat. The little black crow made soft gurgling noises as it gulped down every bit of food with gusto and seemed to beg for more. Grammaw gently laid the baby crow next to Blue, and both of them seemed to snuggle as if they belonged to each other.

As you might guess, Blue was the name we chose for the white-spotted male bird dog that was now in residence, and Blackie was loveable but often a major source of irritation grating on the nerves and patience.

Let me elaborate on the escapades of Blackie and how we finally had an dog named Blue.

Grampaw and Pa searched high and low for the owner of old Blue. They knew in order for old Blue not to hurt the little crow, he had to be a really good bird dog for hunting. In fact he was probably trained to hold a bird without bruising or breaking a bone while retrieving game. A lot of the hill folk told Grampaw and Pa that they would take the dog, but I'm proud to say their answer was no. After about two months of waiting for someone to come forward and claim old Blue, Pa and Grampaw, proudly beaming, said we could keep him. We had been holding our breaths and praying that no one would come take old Blue away. He had stolen our hearts and taken to Grampaw and Pa like glue. His old tail would wag like crazy when one of them approached him and he would lick the daylights out of any uncovered leg or arm. He was the most loveable dog that ever lived and truly a part of our family.

At least Blue wasn't anything like that stupid, old gray goose named Poncho that Grammaw said was better than a watchdog. Blue didn't have a razor-sharp beak and wouldn't bite anything unless it was an old, cold biscuit.

While waiting for someone to claim Blue, Blackie the crow was growing by leaps and bounds. It was because Grammaw fed that crow like he was a condemned prisoner. Every time that crow flapped his cropped little wings, Grammaw was there to poke food down his goozle. That crow would actually make funny little noises, flap his wings in a pitiful state and act like he was starving to death. Anyway, Grammaw wasn't going to ignore this crow, since the crow obviously thought Grammaw was his mother.

After Blackie began to lose his fledgling look, his feathers filled out and he actually looked like a crow. It took him awhile to find out he could fly and then, when he did take flight, we all were like sitting ducks waiting to be whacked! His little crippled foot was like a vise and didn't it deter his determination to inflict bodily harm. In fact, his crippled foot managed to do whatever his brain said to do. I often thought that bird was smarter than the average idiot and had all of us scampering to his every whim.

Because Grampaw, Grammaw, Tut and Baby Jo were staying with us for several weeks until the roof on their home place was repaired from an early spring storm, they naturally settled in our house, as it should have been. We always wanted them to live with us but couldn't convince Grammaw it would be in their best interest. Anyway, for awhile we could be happy knowing they were there with us, making us one very large family.

One morning Grampaw was searching for a special corncob pipe. It wasn't for the corncob bowl, but for the special stem he had bought in town. It had a shiny silver clip that fit snuggly around the bottom and had a perfect fit for the homemade bowls. He was very proud of the new pipe stem because it fit every corncob bowl he ever made. He knew he had placed it on the kitchen table the night before because his pipe was the first object he picked up in the morning as he meandered toward the outhouse. He might not light that pipe until after breakfast but always wanted it either tucked inside his pocket or stuck atop his ear. It would be within his reach if he had a hankerin' to stink up the place.

Grampaw was tearing up the pantry like a madman in search of lost money. He picked up every canned good, turned over iron skillets, lifted up pots and pans, scooted the table sideways, went down in the root cellar beneath the kitchen floor and then let out a spine-tingling screech that made your hair stand on end.

Everyone stood in a row peeking around the person in front of the other, watching Grampaw stomp out the back door, giving the cool morning air a dose of hell fire and brimstone. You could almost see the pitchforks shoot out of his nostrils as he kicked the dirt with his heavy old boots. We knew in an instant that one of us had better find that danged old pipe and stem before Grampaw plowed up the whole back yard with his boots and set the forest on fire with his blistering tongue. We searched every nook and cranny within the house and didn't come up with that pipe. It had vanished like vapor from a boiling pot.

We tried to appease Grampaw in giving him fresh coffee, patting him on top of the head and kissing his stickery, old, whiskered chin. None of those things even made a dent in his temperament. Not wanting to rock the boat or get Grampaw any more riled than he was, we gingerly went about our normal activities and secretly took a peek in places we had already peeked in search of that stupid pipe. It was not to be found. Talk about walking on egg shells; this was going to be a bad day!

Trouble of it was, we were in for more agony. After about two hours of keeping our mouths shut and tiptoeing around the stone-faced, dagger-shooting, lip-pursed, whiskered mountain of a man perched on the chopping block near the smoke house, we saw the back door fling open with a ker-wop and chunks of kindling being rearranged with a vengeance. We knew Ma was on the warpath when she began to re-do things in a forceful manner.

We knew in an instant that something was mighty wrong and we were in for some kind of lecture. Ma never did whack us kids very hard but those black eyes of hers could cut through steel when they began darting like shooting stars. All she had to do when she was on the "outs" with something was to look at us with her sharp, directing glances while standing rigid with her feet spread apart and her hands on her hips doing the Momma sigh! When she did the Momma sigh, releasing hot air in bursts from her lungs, Katie bar the door, you better look out!

One by one, all of us kids began to approach Ma. We had two stone-faced people glaring at us, and with any luck Grammaw and Pa would be the next irate people on a rampage. This family had surely gone bananas and we were caught in the middle of a no-win situation.

Ma looked at Effie Mae and Aunt Sukie and began to give them what for! "Ya best be a gittin' in here! I dun told ya not ta be a messin' with my best thimble. I got all this here mendin' ta do and I don't ritely have a pleasure in rammin' th' needle in my fingers. Iffen ya don't find thet thimble in a hurry, I ain't gonna git them blasted buttons sewed on them shirts!"

Aunt Sukie and Effie Mae protested with all their might. In unison they proclaimed, "But Ma, we ain't been a messin' in yore sewin' chest. Don't'cha remember? Ya was puttin' them patches on Pa's britches th' other day and ya laid it on th' hearth along with the sewin' chest. Ya said not ta touch it whilst ya went to th' check on th' beans ta make sure thay weren't scorchin'. We for shore ain't got thet thimble."

Ma stood there for a few seconds with her mouth gaped open and then proceeded to go back into the house. That was all me and Tut needed and we made a hasty exit before we were singled out for doing something we hadn't done. Me and Tut managed to stay away from all the hullaboo that day and hoped it didn't spill over and drown us the following day.

We were so glad this day had come to an end and delighted that night had arrived. Grampaw and Ma were still fuming and talking about sticky-fingered ghosts roaming the house as they finally went to sleep. It had been an exhausting day for everyone because of a corncob pipe and thimble. Now we had to contend with ghosts. Me and Tut weren't sure about ghosts, but I can tell you right now, we fought them all night.

The next morning, around five o'clock, Grampaw was still hunkered down in bed. It was unusual because he normally was up before the roosters, sitting on the front stoop drinking coffee. Grammaw was in the kitchen squeezing out sourdough biscuits when all of a sudden Grampaw let loose with a loud, "Git outta here!" You could hear a big loud thud as a shoe came flying through the air, pelting the log wall and landing in the front room. Grammaw ran to the bedroom and found Grampaw doctoring his big toe.

"Whut in thunder is th' matter with ya, Grampaw?"

"It's thet damned old crow. Thet critter was pullin' th' hair outta my toe. Afore I knowed whut he was doin' he managed ta jerk my jaw whiskers. I done been attacked by thet mangy old crow. Lookie thar, thar's a chunk of my whiskers layin' on th' floor!"

Grammaw began laughing so hard that tears streamed down her face. She turned away and we heard her say to herself, "Been wantin' sometimes ta do thet myself!" As she walked through the door, me and Tut were peering down from the loft just waiting for the next fiasco.

We had been jolted awake by the thud of the shoe and we honestly thought that the ghosts were coming to claim whatever they wanted. We were relieved to know it was only Grampaw but somehow, we knew this day would be a re-run of the hide and go seek we performed yesterday.

We all sat down to eat our breakfast. The only words spoken was Pa saying Grace. When you have a silent meal, your ears hone in on the sounds of everyone chewing. I'm telling you that people make awful noises. The succession of clickety-clack teeth clamping down on silverware, food swishing around inside the mouth, the gullets gulping down coffee and bits of food makes the inside of your mouth crawl and grates on the nerves. Whatever had to be done, we needed to find Grampaws pipe and Ma's thimble.

After we had finished eating our breakfast, all of us kids decided to search every nook and cranny until we found the missing items. It didn't take very long before the searching came to an abrupt end.

Aunt Sukie was running toward the barn as her long blond hair, tied loosely with a bright red ribbon, was flowing in the breeze. Out of nowhere came Blackie! He dived at Aunt Sukie, hooked his claws into her hair and jerked the ribbon right out of her hair, taking part of her hair with it. She was screaming bloody murder and doing a solo two-step dance.

Pa, already in the barn, watched Blackie as he flew into the barn with the ribbon. Blackie swooped up into the loft and deposited the ribbon into a clump of hay. Then, Blackie flew out of the barn and perched himself atop the chicken house. Pa climbed the loft ladder and found a stash of goodies hidden in cracks and under hay. Pa picked everything up and headed toward the house. Pa yelled for everyone to come into the kitchen. There they were, Grampaw's corncob pipe and shiny pipe stem, Ma's thimble, a handful of marbles, goose feathers, a fork, two nickels, a bright red ribbon, a spool of thread, pieces of Grammaw's quilting material and some of Grampaw's whiskers.

After we all had a good laugh, we were relieved to know that Blackie was the sticky-fingered, night roaming ghostly bird with a penchant for brightly colored objects. We couldn't stop Blackie from taking things he liked any more than we could stop the sun from coming up in the morning, but at least we knew where to find "lost" items and how to take things in stride when one of us was displaced by his antics.

Blue was always called "Blue." He was a great quail hunting dog and we loved him to death. However, Blackie's name was changed to Blackeena when she had two baby crows the following year. As for us, well, we got used to having things disappear. To find some of the lost items, all we had to do was say a prayer and try to follow the ghostly, sticky-fingered black crows in the air with the aid of our beloved, old friend Blue.

Epilogue

While Daddy and I shared many mornings together and laughed as he told his stories, I could tell that Daddy was slowly sinking away and becoming increasingly slower with his speech. His attitude and zest for life had waned and his thought processes had become even more confused.

One morning, I decided to go to the nursing home an hour earlier. When I got there, Daddy wasn't feeling very well. He wasn't as alert and was having difficulty staying awake. Dementia and diabetes had reached an all-time high and were trying to consume the remaining portion of Daddy, a once robust, vigorous, handsome and charming man. It was a wake-up call for me, in that life is but a fleeting moment of precious thoughts and treasures taken away to be stored in an eternal passageway among those who have gone before us to prepare the way. It shouldn't be a fearful time, but one for rejoicing in homecomings for people who we have loved and cherished.

I immediately paged the nurse. After the nurse had examined Daddy, she told me he needed to be hospitalized. His vital signs needed to be monitored for twenty-four hours. Since the nursing home was within walking distance to the local hospital, Daddy was wheeled to the emergency room.

As I waited for the doctor to advise me about Daddy, I remembered an earlier conversation with Daddy. His words kept rolling around in my mind "I bet I've told you more than thirty stories. What are you going to do with all those stories?"

"I'm going to write a book, Daddy, about you and your stories."

"A book! Why, those old stories aren't more than a half page long. You can't write a book with just a few pages of notes scribbled down on a piece of paper."

There was a long silent pause before Daddy resumed the conversation. "You mean you actually want someone to read about my stories?" Daddy said as tears welled up in his steel gray eyes and gently dropped down his cheeks. "I always wanted to write a book to keep my stories alive but I never got around to it. Just never seemed to find the time."

"Oh yes, Daddy, they're wonderful stories and I want people to see, hear and feel your childhood antics, know about your wild imagination and relive your zany escapades through your words. It's a wonderful legacy, a treasure for the heart and I intend to write a book."

"Try to do one thing for me, okay? If you can write one book, do you think you can write two? Never tell anyone about everything you know, especially everything at one time. That's how I came to be known as 'Windy John.' I kept them guessing! Promise me you'll keep my stories alive."

My Daddy died in August of 1995.

I promise, Daddy, I promise…

* * *